Around the Corner with Paradise

Book 5 in the Paradise series

Carol Ann Cole

Around the Corner with Paradise

Cover image: Nicole Ruuska
Cover design: Rebekah Wetmore
Editor: Andrew Wetmore

ISBN: 978-1-990187-92-6
First edition August, 2023

2475 Perotte Road
Annapolis County, NS
B0S 1A0

moosehousepress.com
info@moosehousepress.com

We live and work in Mi'kma'ki, the ancestral and unceded territory of the Mi'kmaw people. This territory is covered by the "Treaties of Peace and Friendship" which Mi'kmaw and Wolastoqiyik (Maliseet) people first signed with the British Crown in 1725. The treaties did not deal with surrender of lands and resources but in fact recognized Mi'kmaq and Wolastoqiyik (Maliseet) title and established the rules for what was to be an ongoing relationship between nations. We are all Treaty people.

Also by Carol Ann Cole

The *Paradise* Series

Paradise
Paradise 548
Paradise on the Morrow*
Paradise d'Entremont Private Investigator*

Other fiction

Less Than Innocent* (co-author)

Non-fiction

Comfort Heart—a Personal Memoir (with Anjali Kapoor)
Lessons Learned Upside the Head
If I Knew Then What I Know Now
From the Heart (with Deanna Jones)
Learning to Slow Dance with Footprints of Kindness* (coming in 2024)

*from Moose House Publications

This book is dedicated to my dear friend Doreen Foss, with thanks for the many teachable moments and the memories, both past and present. Thank you for being my trusted confidante.

Around the Corner with Paradise

1: Ben who?

Thomas carried the coffee pot to the family's favourite window seat, where his wife of twelve hours sat facing him with cup in hand and a smile on her face. "Good morning my love. You made our coffee rather quickly...very impressive."

"I can't take credit for the coffee this morning," Paradise said. "I suspect Hope is the one who prepared our coffee and also altered the timer, knowing we might sleep in given the late hour last night when she left."

Thomas filled his own coffee cup and returned the pot to the kitchen before sitting down beside his bride. He loved how Paradise leaned into him whenever they sat together on the window seat.

"Thomas, you did hang in there with the kids much later than I expected you would on our wedding night." Paradise was smiling as she spoke. "I assume it had something to do with Ben hanging around Hope? He certainly did help with the clean-up and he did a good job, honey. He tried so hard to make a good first impression."

"My decision on first impressions includes Ben...or whatever his name is...having kept his word when he walked Hope over to Eugenie and Pops'. I wanted to walk her over myself, but she gave me one of those '*Dad*' looks, so I backed off. I asked Ben to walk Hope to the door, but under no circumstances was he to go inside. Even if Eugenie and Pops came to the door and begged him to come inside he was to refuse and high-tail it home to wherever he was staying. He gave me his word."

Paradise hugged her husband as she spoke. "Sounds like some pretty specific guidelines last night. By the way, Hope called while you were in the shower to share that Pops had been standing in the doorway, leaning on the door frame, as if he had been tipped off that they were on their way over. She really did want to tip us off, just in case we see Ben walking by this morning, that Pops invited him to join the three of them for breakfast."

"Yes, I did call Pops last night to tell him I lost the war of words and therefore I wouldn't be the one walking Hope over to spend the night. I asked him to watch for them because it shouldn't take very long...a few minutes actually...before he would be able to see her."

Turning to Paradise, Thomas continued, "Christ, I know she's only a few days away from her sixteenth birthday, but he looks like mid-twenties, don't you think?"

"No, he is not mid-twenties, Thomas. Ben is nineteen. I asked him myself when you were busy laying down the rules with Hope."

Taking his hand, Paradise continued, "I wasn't going to raise the elephant in the room during our brief, two-day, honeymoon, Thomas. But I'm certain we are both thinking back to when you were nineteen and it was my sixteenth birthday weekend and we made love, and Hope was born nine months later."

"Roger that." Thomas couldn't put his words together. He was deep in thought, reflecting on some sixteen years ago. Not only had he taken the virginity of a fifteen-year-old girl, but also, when Paradise chose God over him, he left her minutes after they made love. To add insult to injury, he left town in the pre-dawn of the next morning. Not his finest hour on many counts.

"You know I'm not big on looking back, Thomas, but it was very easy last night, when we watched Ben and our little girl dance to our song—*Our song*—to see why we would do that in the moment."

"So you understand that I—"

Paradise interrupted Thomas mid-sentence. "I wasn't finished, honey. This is important. I want you to know that I have had many talks with our girl about her changing body. She is totally comfortable with these discussions and I promise you Hope and I will be having another talk very soon. That's all you need to know other than don't worry. Hope and I have got this!"

"Sure," said Thomas as he pulled Paradise onto his lap and wrapped his arms around her.

At that precise moment, and the moment was still early—9:55 am on the first day of their two-day honeymoon—a commotion could be heard at the back door.

As the door opened, the commotion turned into a hurricane. At full speed, Lee appeared, with a rather sheepish-looking Denis and Waine right behind.

"We're not staying," said Denis. "You have my word."

"I just need my new fishing pole and then we're gone," Lee said.

Pointing at Denis and Waine, he continued, "My uncles said if I don't sit my ass down on a chair but just come in long enough to get my fishing pole they would take me fishing right now. We have to get the worms first, though. Am I right, Uncle Denis? Uncle Waine?"

Lee had started addressing every comment to both of his uncles. For now, they found it both humorous and delightful.

Denis jumped in. "Paradise, I saw your eyebrow go up when Lee swore. Lee, what did we say about using a swear word? About using *any* swear words?"

"I think you said we shouldn't swear, but when we are just three guys in the cottage, it won't matter if we slip up a bit. It was my fault, Mummy, and I'm sorry, and we're off to the fishing pond."

And the hurricane was gone as fast as it had appeared. Denis and Waine shrugged and followed Lee out.

All was forgiven.

2: Breakfast interventions

"Good morning, Ben, come on in," Hope said. "My grandparents are busy with 'preparations.' To be more specific, Eugenie is making breakfast and Pops is reviewing his twenty questions for you. Consider yourself warned."

She opened the door wide and made a grand gesture for Ben to enter.

Pops and Eugenie were working together in the kitchen preparing what appeared to be a feast. Ben assumed others were joining them and maybe he was a bit early. "I hope I'm not ahead of myself this morning? I couldn't wait to see you again, Hope, and meet some of your family."

So far Eugenie and Pops had not even turned around to acknowledge Ben was in the house.

Pops was the one who turned away from the stove first. "Ben, believe me when I say you will meet the entire family *today*, especially if you have plans to see our Hope. However, let's keep that talk for a bit...until we're enjoying our breakfast and each other's company. Are those flowers for us Ben? Here, let me take them from you and pour you a coffee so you and Hope can sit while we do the hard work over the stove."

Pops knew exactly where they kept the only two vases they owned. He often surprised Eugenie with flowers. He knew she liked one vase better than the other. It was kind of a mauve-coloured glass but he had long ago forgotten exactly what that type of glass was called.

Pops figured his intelligence and his capacity to grow had sure improved since he met Eugenie. Knowing what different kinds of vases were made of didn't interest him much, though.

"There's no '*we*' in this preparation, my love," Eugenie said with a chuckle. "Kids, I'm making French toast, crisping the bacon and putting it in the warming oven for a second or two. Hope, honey, there is a fruit salad in the icebox. Could you take that out for me and put it in the centre of the table, please."

"No problem, Eugenie. And, Pops, don't you dare start with your helter-skelter list of questions for Ben. I want to hear your questions as well as Ben's answers for everything."

Turning to Ben, Hope continued, "It will be fun so don't bolt on us, okay?"

"Not on your life, Hope. I'm right where I want to be with nothing to hide. I'm comfortable with questions all day long, if that will make your family a bit more pleased to see me around."

"Ah, now that you have your coffee in hand I'll throw out my first question," Pops said. "Our young lady, Hope, is turning sixteen in a few weeks and you would be how old?"

"I'm nineteen, sir."

"You seem older. You act older, somehow. You better be telling me the truth." Pops seemed to want a fight.

Hope wasn't sure how long this breakfast would last. She looked at Ben, who didn't seem uncomfortable at all. In fact, he looked lovely...just plain lovely. She really did want to date Ben...as his girlfriend. Hope had never been anyone's girlfriend and along comes a beautiful stranger who is interested in her!

"I *am* nineteen, sir. Would you like to see my driver's license?" Ben was trying to calm down. He was boiling mad inside. He had already told Hope's parents how old he was and he was pretty sure they would have shared that news with Pops.

"Our house is relatively small," Eugenie said. "I'm not listening on purpose, Ben and Pops, but it sounds to me like you two are circling each other, itching for a fight. There will be none of that in our home."

After placing the last of the food platters on the table, and topping up everyone's coffee, Eugenie asked everyone to bow their heads in prayer before digging in. She figured that might keep the 'ugly' out of the conversation for now.

"God, we thank you for this beautiful breakfast before us, and for watching over Pops and Ben in particular, since they don't seem to like each other very much. They're jealous of each other I believe but you leave that with me...I've got it covered. We thank you for our health and our little home. Amen."

Hope, Eugenie and Pops were on their second helping of French toast and Ben was on his third. The bacon was long gone along with the fruit salad.

"You sure can eat, boy. Isn't anyone feeding you while you're in our village? How long have you been here? Where are you staying? When are you leaving? Why are you here in the first place? I thought I knew everyone around here, but it seems you've proved me wrong. Over to you or as those smart business people like to say, 'the floor is all yours.'" Pops tabled all of his questions at once, but he felt some good about getting them all out. He wasn't so sure Hope agreed with his presentation, but it was too late now.

Hope opened her mouth to say something, but Ben reached over and squeezed her hand. "I believe your Pops gave me the floor. Don't worry, I don't mind at all."

He took one final swig of his coffee and began. "I grew up in Paris, France. Actually, and because I suspect you might check my facts Pops, I grew up just on the *outskirts of Paris* in what they call a quintessentially French town."

Pushing his license across the table, Ben left it directly in front of Pops. "Chantilly is a pretty town and growing up there I was a happy child with everything to look forward to. We have bars, tons of French restaurants, lots of gift shops because we do receive a lot of visitors who dare to venture outside of Paris. We also have a wonderful Chateau housing the second largest art collection in France. My mother and I used to love spending afternoons there, waiting for father to return from his job."

It was Eugenie who was first to interrupt. Pops would later say it was her soft skills that alerted her to something Ben said. She put her hand over Ben's. "You speak of your parents as if they are perhaps no longer around, or is it that they are no longer in your life? Not here with you perhaps?"

As Ben began to weep, Pops wondered if he was wrong about his wife's soft skills. Something was wrong and he was embarrassed for their young guest who was obviously trying to impress, especially Hope.

"That's it. Let's go for a walk, Ben," Hope said with tears in her eyes as she glared at Eugenie and Pops.

"No, honestly, it's okay, Hope, but I appreciate you coming to my defence. I've got this and I figure if I can win these two over I might win you over as well."

If you only knew, thought Hope.

Ben started again. "I am an only child. My parents were and are everything to me. They shared a love match made in heaven. My mother taught me from the time I was very young the importance of treating women well." Ben smiled at Hope as he said this. He had more to say.

"In my final year at university, and, before you ask, I studied Fine Arts, my parents came to the campus one weekend to start taking some of my things back home. I entered university at a very young age, barely sixteen, and had accumulated way too much stuff in my tiny dorm room. I did have a car but would never be able to get everything back home in one trip."

Ben took a deep breath. Eugenie asked if he would like a glass of cold water. He took his time drinking it and wondered if anyone realized he was stalling for time.

No one interrupted so he continued.

3: Eight Cape St. Mary Road

"My parents left the campus very late that day," Ben said. "We were all exhausted but it had been a wonderful day. I would be leaving the campus for good this time and with a degree in my hand...all thanks to my mother and father. I went to bed the second they left, not even knowing what time it was.

"When someone knocked on my dorm room door, I was sound asleep, and had no idea how much time had passed. On the other side of the door were two policemen and a priest who had the sad task of telling me both of my parents were killed in a car collision not far from our home in Chantilly."

The room was very quiet. After a moment, Ben continued. "I later learned the grim details...a drunken driver hit my mom and dad head-on. They were both killed upon impact. In a second my family was gone. The other driver was charged with multiple counts of various things, but that's not important this morning. What's important is what I learned from the contents of my parents' will. And I'm jumping around here, but after my parents' funeral I couldn't stay in our home. At least not initially. I returned and finished my final year at the University of Paris. A busload, literally a busload, of my friends made the trek to Chantilly for the funeral. For the rest of my life, I will remember my friends; one by one and all dressed in black, getting off that school bus in front of our church. I learned later they had discussed how they would dip their heads as they saw me standing by the hearse and hoped it would convey they were all right there with me. That's what helped me return to my dorm room only a week after the funeral."

Looking around the kitchen table, Ben realized he had to hurry this story up. Hope and her grandparents looked sad and exhausted. That's how Ben felt as well. "I'm almost finished so if you don't mind I'll continue. I've never told this story in its entirety and I find it very emotional to revisit all of it at one time." There had been no need to voice the details while he was still in Chantilly, because everyone for miles around attended the funeral.

Ben wondered if he should have come for breakfast after all. He was surprised at how emotional he felt. "I had been back home for a week or so when my father's legal team called and asked me to come in for the reading of the will. Or they could come to me if I would prefer that. I did, and so on a sombre morning, they thanked me for the coffee and the business of the will took place. I was an only child, so it was no surprise that everything was left to me.

"I had no idea my parents had accumulated such wealth, but what's important to this conversation is that I inherited a small cottage...drum role, please...at #8 Cape St Mary Road! I am currently the proud owner of the rather tattered home where the highway and Cape St Mary Road meet. You've likely seen it a million times as you pass by. It's in bad shape but I'm here to fix it up and live in it for now. My father was handy with all types of home repairs so I learned from the best. Don't get me wrong...I'll need help, but right now I don't know what I don't know about the house, so I'll find an expert to check it over. Asking for help is not beneath me."

As Ben smiled, Hope thought it might be the most beautiful smile she had ever seen.

"I have already driven up the line to check out a few French courses at your beautiful French university. I figure my Parisian French might need a bit of an adjustment, and I'm keen to learn that level of detail. I've been here for a few weeks but have kept to myself outside of my daily walks on Mavillette beach. That's where I met a couple of rather large boys from Hawaii and we got to talking about your parents' wedding, Hope, and they thought it might be okay if I joined in. When I saw you in your red dress I knew I had to meet you. Can I stop there for now? Please?"

Ben was smiling at Hope, who agreed instantly that he need not share any further details at the moment. After all, her parents would need to hear the whole story, and Paradise and Thomas were on their honeymoon until tomorrow.

"That damn red dress is no more than a slip," Pops said, "and if I had had my way you would have changed before you came downstairs all slinky like."

Pops was serious so Eugenie added her thoughts. "All slinky like? Really, my love?" She was enjoying this. "With all this young lady had on her list for her parents' wedding day, planning everything down to the last second, not to mention the last dance, it's the red dress you want to talk about?"

Eugenie took Hope's hands in her own and finished her thought. "Hope, yesterday was one of the most beautiful days I have ever been part of. With all your parents have endured to be together I cried my eyes out the entire day...with love. Ben, you mentioned your parents shared a true love story, so wait until Hope tells you her parents' love story. Honestly, you won't believe it. All true, though."

Eugenie was crying again. She moved her chair closer to Hope and gave her a big hug. "I'm so proud of you, sweetheart. And I totally approve of the slinky red dress."

"Eugenie," Ben said, "please let Hope and me do the dishes and clean your kitchen up after all the work you have done to fill our bellies. You go and do something. and take Pops with you."

Grabbing Eugenie's hand, Pops spoke up. "We won't be long, kids. We're just going over to the intersection where our highway and Cape St Mary Road meet. I want to see what kind of a job you've got ahead of you, Ben."

Not sure if Pops was serious but Ben shouted as they left the house, "Door's open so take a good look around and inside too. Don't mind the pots on the floor. They catch the rain coming in through the roof."

4: Down my throat?

"Let's work while we talk. Is that okay with you?" Hope was so nervous she didn't know what to say. She really liked Ben and didn't want to screw this up.

She felt like such a kid beside Ben. Nineteen, and a university graduate! *He must be some smart*, she thought as she watched Ben roll up his shirtsleeves and tackle the pile of dishes.

"My God, how long has it been since Eugenie did her dishes?" Ben said, laughing. "Look at the pots and pans."

"Don't you let Eugenie hear you even kid about the cleanliness of her kitchen. She prides herself in keeping it spotless at all times. Everyone says you can eat off of her floors and I tend to believe that. I have dusted her home on occasion for her and I can't find a speck of dust or much of anything to clean up. She grew up in a convent. Bet you didn't know that, and my mom was in a convent too for five years, starting on her sixteenth birthday. And, I was born in the convent nine months later. Does any of this shock you, Ben?"

"Not at all. It opens the door to knowing you even better and deeper. Do you have a boyfriend? Or is that impolite of me to ask? See how I just threw that in there?"

"I do not. Do you have a girlfriend?"

"If I did, do you think I would have held you as close as I did during the last dance last night?"

"That does not answer my question," said Hope, and she looked worried all of a sudden.

"No, I do *not* have a girlfriend back in Paris. I dated during my university days but nothing that got serious. I haven't dated since my parents were killed. I'm depressed about it, to be honest, Hope and I am trying very hard to work through my grief, my anger and God knows what else."

Thinking he might have said too much Ben put his arms around Hope and was relieved that she put her arms around him.

"How can I help you?" Hope spoke in a whisper.

"You just did." Ben was content to hold his new friend tight and stroke her long silky hair. He could get lost in her hair. "When do you think the interrogation police will be back?"

Hope pulled away and gave him a playful slap on the shoulder. "It wouldn't surprise me if they stopped at Mom and Dad's place, even though everyone has been asked to respect their two-day honeymoon and leave them alone. If they stopped, they've invited the honeymooners to accompany them to the break and enter that was about to take place at number eight."

While she was talking, Ben put a hand on either side of Hope's face and brought her mouth to his. He didn't think she would mind, and if she did, he would change her mind.

Opening his mouth he encouraged her to do the same so they could explore each other. Mistake. *Big mistake.*

"Oh. My. Good. God. Almighty. Are you really trying to stick your tongue down my throat right now?" Hope was yelling. "Is this how it's done between couples? Do you stick your tongue down every girl's throat when you kiss her? This is what I've got to look for-ward to?"

Hope knew she was being over-dramatic but she wasn't done yet, and she could see that Ben knew this about her already. "My first kiss, and that's how you kiss me? Well, technically, I've kissed a girl, but this is what counts...boy and girl...this is what I want. But not the way you want it, apparently."

"Hope, I'm sorry. I'm so sorry. I have wanted to kiss you for almost twenty-four hours and I didn't think you would object. Was I wrong to think that? Tell me..."

"I've never kissed a boy before, and I hope you won't laugh at this, but I don't want to be like my mother and have a kid when I'm sixteen. I can hardly look after myself some days and I don't think I would make a good girlfriend if that's what you want, Ben. Is it?"

"Listen to me, Hope. I know I'm older, and at our age three years is a lifetime. I'm sorry I kissed you. If it happens again it will be because you reached out to kiss me. Understood?"

"Roger that," was all Hope said in reply.

"And for the record, I think you would make a wonderful girlfriend. You don't have to worry about having a 'kid', as you called it, because I have a lifetime of things to accomplish before I find a wife, get married and have children. And I bet you have at least as many goals, and maybe more. We got off to a bad start, so forget the kiss and let's go and sit outside and watch for Eugenie and Pops. Come on."

Ben put Hope's hand in his and they walked outside to sit on the stoop.

"I'm embarrassed to have overreacted, Ben, and I'm hoping you can forget it."

"I will never forget the kiss, but I promise to forget the 'baby nine months later' part and the warning that you wouldn't make a good girlfriend. I'll focus on the kiss. How does that sound?"

"Sure."

Hope decided Ben would be hearing one-word answers from her. For now.

5: Badass uncles

"Well," Denis said, "you might not want to head back to the cabin yet, young man, but if Uncle Waine and I told you we have a major gift for you, I bet you would say, 'Take me to the cabin, boys.' Am I right, Lee?"

"I have to be a major? What does that mean?" Lee did not want to go back to the cabin. He liked driving around with his new uncles.

"Sorry, Lee," Waine said. "Your Uncle Denis was trying to be fancy with his all-uptown talk. He should have just said we have a gift back at the cabin that we think you will like. It's something the three of us can do together. What do you think, should we turn this car around and head back? We've been driving around for quite some time."

"Yes please turn around and take me to your cabin," came the small voice from the back seat. "Can you give me a hint? Do you know what a hint is?"

Before Denis or Waine could respond, Lee described his version of a hint. "A hint is kind of like when you tell me what my gift is even if you don't want to. So, are you going to tell me?"

"No hints," Waine said. "However, I will tell you that we bought your gift in Hawaii so we didn't even know you and we were already buying gifts for you. Crazy, right?"

"Getting presents is never crazy. It's my favourite thing. Can I have it as soon as we jump out of the car?"

Denis enjoyed listening to this exchange. Waine was very engaged with Lee and this gave him something to focus on. Something he could be happy about. This would be good for Wayne's mental health. Denis was relieved.

Looking at Lee, Denis said, "Lee, this is going to make you a badass just like your uncles. What do you think of that?"

"If you tell my mother that you called me a badass you would get such trouble. We better make it a secret and only call each other a badass when my mother is not with me. I'm not kidding, I don't know what she would do to punish me but I bet she would also punish you guys. Even though you're both tons bigger than my mom, I bet she would do something to punish you. For sure, I would get so much trouble."

Denis and Waine had carefully hung Lee's brilliant red boxing gloves over the chair closest to the door. He would see the gloves the second the door was unlocked. They had left their own gloves back in Hawaii, but they were relatively certain they could take Lee on even with his shiny new gloves.

Memories are made of this, thought Denis. He had heard Paradise use the expression and decided it was worth remembering. Maybe he would even use the expression one day. Done!

6: It's 4 pm somewhere

"Now I've seen everything. I swear to God I just saw pizza delivered via a hot-looking rental car." Pops was out of his car and over to Eugenie's side to open her door. Ben and Hope smiled from the stoop.

"I kid you not. Hope, you have told everyone to leave Paradise and Thomas alone for at least the weekend, yet we just watched two big, burly men peel themselves out of a little sports car that they can't possibly be comfortable in."

"They sure are handsome men, though," Eugenie added.

Hope was on her feet. "Oh. My. God. I told Clint and Jim Taylor to come back today with enough pizza to feed the Cape. They're the Canadian arm of Private Investigators Unlimited. I followed them out of the house because I thought they looked suspicious and they let me totally embarrass myself before telling me who they are. They kept trying to inch their way to the bride and groom, then I observed them lean in and chat with each other before making a hasty exit via the back door. I felt like I was chasing them away, but given that they hadn't made it to their target couple, we decided it would be a wonderful surprise kept for today. They said they would come back for breakfast, but I suggested they leave Paradise and Thomas alone until around 4pm, so they do follow instructions fairly well."

Hope knew she was rambling. She jumped up and gave instructions to Ben, Eugenie and Pops as she began running home. "I want the three of you to follow me, but give me ten or fifteen minutes to deal with this and make sure my parents are okay with post-wedding-day pizza all around!"

Ben was heading for his car, saying, "I'll drive you, Hope. Please wait for me."

But she was long-gone.

It was Eugenie's turn to speak up. "Ben, when Thomas learns you have a car he will not be impressed, so driving Hope home is a bad idea. Come on in and chat with us about your cute little home and we will share how Pops came to have a newly-built home just after his was bulldozed. The only thing left was part of the façade..."

Pops couldn't hold his tongue for another second. "Ben, I didn't even know what the word 'façade' meant. I just knew I was losing my home. I didn't get to pick the side of my house that we would protect. We saved the side with the least amount of rot, to be honest. It's a great story for another day. Today, it's all about you, young man. Starting with your Cape home." Pops had a million ideas but he knew Ben would have a million more.

"I'm thinking everyone in the big house, especially Thomas, will want all the details about your house, Ben. Let's take our time, but head over before Hope returns to fetch us." Eugenie spoke so softly the men could hardly hear her.

"Eugenie, what's wrong with your voice, honey? You never talk like that." Pops wondered if he was a wee bit jealous of the beautiful stranger who had yet to misstep.

"Drive over with us, Ben. Pops might need to grill you a bit more."

Eugenie hugged Pops just in case this was bothering him a bit more than he was able to admit.

7: The honeymoon is over

Thomas and his bride spent a leisurely morning in bed, followed by brunch on Mavillette beach. They had just returned home and were enjoying the shower when the doorbell rang.

Laughing, Thomas said, "Take your time, sweetheart. I'll get the door."

So much for two days alone, he thought as he stepped into yesterday's pants and went downstairs two steps at a time. He could see a mountain of pizza boxes, but for some reason the delivery folks were hiding their faces behind the boxes.

He opened the door and tried to get a better look at the men in front of him, but Thomas was stumped. "Wrong address, I'm afraid, boys. Believe me, I did not order eight boxes of pizza, but I'll tell you what I will do. I'll pay double for just one box. Is that possible or no?"

"I can't do this," came from one of the two men.

"On three, we drop the boxes. Just to waist level though. One. Two. Three."

Thomas recognized Clint and Jim but he couldn't believe his eyes.

"Congratulations, man! Are you going to invite us in? These boxes are hot and getting heavier by the minute."

"Hot and heavy is what you just interrupted boys, but, sure, come on in," said Thomas as he laughed and reached out to help with the boxes.

"What in God's name are you doing here and what made you think you should arrive with eight boxes of pizza?

"We were following orders given to us by a red slinky dress and I forget who was wearing it."

"Don't you even joke about that or, so help me God—"

Hope interrupted them. "Sorry. Sorry. Sorry. Dad, I meant to get over here earlier and fill you in. These two were at the back of the living room yesterday and when we determined you and mom had not seen them, we made a joint decision and they left to check in and have a bit of time to themselves after their long trip to join us."

"Believe me, if Hope hadn't intervened we would have been here at around nine this morning."

"Thank you, Hope," said Thomas, giving his daughter a big hug.

"Well, don't thank me just yet. Soon, very soon I suspect, we will be joined by Denis, Waine, Lee, Wilmot and Marie, and Ben, too, if that's okay. He's coming over with Pops and Eugenie."

"And so it begins," said Thomas as Paradise drifted down the stairs looking beautiful in a new sundress, or at least one he didn't remember seeing before.

Catching his stare and the raising of one eyebrow, Paradise said, "Don't worry, my love, it's new and you are seeing it for the first time."

Paradise turned around so her husband could see the nearly-there back of her dress. Turning to Clint and Jim she offered hugs all around...and saved her biggest hug for her daughter.

"Hope, thank you again for the incredible work you put in to give us a perfect wedding and reception, right down to the last dance. And the way you kicked everyone out at the end was as magical as the day had been."

"Mom, hold that thought because the hurricane we call Lee just dove out of the car and is flying toward the door."

Hope bent down to grab him saying, "Hey, brother, good to see you and what do you have on your hands? My goodness, what could this be? Very pretty colour, too. I love red."

"You don't even know, do you, Hope?" Lee loved this. "Mom, dad, do you know what I have on my hands?"

"Where are your manners, Lee?" His mother spoke first. "You are blocking the doorway so your uncles can't even get in the house. Come on, let's get you inside so you can show us a few of your boxing moves."

"Ah, you know what I'm wearing on my hands, right, mom? I was hoping you'd be like Hope and not even know what they are."

Thomas decided to wade in. "Lee, I'm pretty sure your sister knows exactly what you have on your hands. And all taped up, I see. This is serious stuff right here." Thomas looked at Denis and Waine and offered a silent thank you.

"No. You heard Hope ask me what I had on my hands, right, daddy?"

"Yes, I did, son. She was offering you the chance to tell her all about your bright red boxing gloves..."

Thomas was interrupted with, "Actually, they are brilliant red not bright red, dad."

8: Lee's confusion

Hope motioned everyone to move inside. "I see Ben, Pops and Eugenie coming so I'll wait for them to park the car."

"Of course you will," her dad said with a smile. Thomas wanted to ask what Ben was doing with the family again today, but he wasn't sure he wanted to hear the answer.

"Pops, did you like Ben's home here?"

"It's more like a cottage, I think," said Eugenie.

"Hey, let me answer that question for you," Ben said. "Currently it's a rotting, beaten-down cottage on the verge of a total collapse. However, the foundation is solid (yes, a professional told me that and I have the papers to prove it) and I will turn it into my Cape St Mary home." He was clearly proud of his inheritance.

"Pops, it's not lost on me that you haven't answered Hope's question. Tell me honestly, what do you think of it?"

"All in good time, son. Today's about the bride and groom and I suspect some pretty good carpenters and even house builders will be here later, so stay close to me. I'll make all the introductions."

"Pops is in your corner, Ben, so that's a very good start." Hope was obviously anxious for Ben to be welcomed into her family.

"That's one down and the rest of your family to go, Hope. Clearly, your Pops is well loved by all."

"He sure is, and everyone really listens to him. I've seen it happen. I should go and touch base with my mom and dad. I see Clint and Jim Taylor here and I want to make sure mom and dad understand why they left yesterday only to return today with what looks like a mountain of boxes of pizza. You're okay on your own for a few minutes?"

"You go, girl, and I'll try to manage without you." Ben was laughing as he kissed Hope's hand before releasing it.

Out of the corner of his eye, Ben saw the young boy he believed to be Hope's brother heading his way. This could be trouble, or this could be one more person in his corner.

"Do you know who I am?" Lee was trying for his most ugly and dangerous look.

Ben was trying very hard not to laugh out loud, and thankfully he managed to hold it together. "I don't believe we've been introduced. I'm Ben."

Lee looked at the stranger's extended hand but he didn't want to shake it so he kept talking. "Is my sister hurt? Did you do something to make her sad?"

With some alarm Ben looked around to see if Hope was indeed hurt. He watched her hug her parents and laugh, then turned back to the youngster. "Your sister is laughing with her parents and some other guests, so I don't think she's been hurt. I still don't know your name."

"My name is Lee and I saw, with my own eyes, that you kissed my sister's hand to make it better. What were you making better?"

"Sometimes, Lee, you see a man kiss a woman's hand because he is going to miss her every second they are apart. Does that make sense to you?"

Ben was able to hold himself together and he could see that Lee was very seriously thinking about what he just said.

"Oh. My. God. That's what my sister says when something crazy happens. Do you even know Hope? You're not going to be her boyfriend, are you? You should know that my father and I do not want Hope to have a boyfriend. I hear daddy say that to her all the time. I don't think he's joking, either, so you better watch it."

Ben was enjoying this way too much and Lee was on a roll. Ben was anxious to hear what Hope's brave brother would say next.

Lee did not disappoint. "Mr. Ben, I should warn you that I'm a trained boxer. Well, I'm getting' trained to be a boxer. I have two uncles who are badass boxers, so make sure you don't mess with them. No telling my mom that I swore, either. If you tell her, I'll get trouble and my uncles won't like that one little bit." Lee looked around to make sure he could see his uncles and they could see him, too.

"It sounds like you have bodyguards, so I'll make sure I don't get into any trouble at all. I box a bit, too, Lee, is there a boxing club anywhere around?"

"Sure is. Can't you see it? It's right over there. Cabin #3."

9: Whispering Hope

Hope sat on the window seat, lost in thought, pencil poised to write but not sure what she wanted to say.

She relived the moment during the wedding party when she had been nervous as she approached the lovely lady who had appeared to be a bit stuck-up, with her ramrod-straight back. Hope offered her champagne for a toast to the happy couple.

She remembered every word of their exchange because she found Doctor Scott fascinating. She was smart and so sure of herself. Hope liked that. Especially in women like her mom and the doctor.

"I believe I have the advantage of knowing who you are, since I ticked each guest off as they came inside our very crowded home that is all dressed up for Thomas and Paradise's wedding day." Hope had been so nervous she thought she might be sick. At least that would stop her from rambling. "You're Doctor Scott, I believe?" She extended a hand offering a glass of bubbly.

"You are correct, Hope, and may I congratulate you on hosting this day for your parents, clipboard in hand, and picking each of us out as we stepped inside your home. Your parents will be very proud of how you orchestrated their special day. Today you can call me Sydney. When you are in my offices you might try 'Doctor Scott'."

Hope thought she even smiled as she said that. Maybe just a tiny smile.

"Bring your inside voice with you. I have grown accustomed to silence while I work. If you don't have an inside voice, perhaps you could whisper?" This was said with another smile, and Hope felt she could finally breathe.

Having told her mother that Sydney said it would be possible for her to see where she worked, Hope wanted to go to the big city right away. Sydney didn't offer the invitation quite as strongly as Hope remembered it but she desperately wanted to go.

Death. Morgue. Autopsy.

It excited Hope in a way she could not put into words. Could this be what she wanted to study after she finished high school? University...probably lots of university.

Thomas and Paradise were talking work stuff over coffee early one morning. Hope was listening quietly, waiting for the right time to interrupt. Her brother was still sleeping, so the house was quiet...she wasn't eavesdropping.

"Mom, can I go to Halifax with you, please? Sydney invited me when we talked at your wedding. She said she would be happy to show me around all of her offices, including the morgue where her dead folks are. She used different words and I'm learning what they mean from my Encyclopedias as I go. I read stuff from two of them last night." Hope refilled her parents' coffee cups before joining them at the kitchen table with her own glass of juice.

"The answer to your question is 'no', sweetheart. I hate to ruin that beautiful smile that has already left your face, but I believe you will understand when I give you some detail, and I will give you as much information as possible without breaking a promise to Sydney. I promised her that I would not share details of this project with anyone, other than Thomas, who is in this one with me. She hired both of us."

Paradise saw the perfect example of how her girl was maturing when she didn't either storm away from the table or say her mother never let her do anything. "I'm listening, mother."

"Your father and I have signed two separate contracts with Sydney. In fact, one is with 'Sydney' and the other is with, 'Doctor Sydney Scott.' My trip to Halifax this time is to meet with Sydney, at her home. That's how personal this is. I promise to share all the details if and when I am able to do that, honey. I will just say that Sydney's heart is breaking while she is reliving a nightmare that she was forced to live through when she was roughly your age. Can you trust me enough to leave it at that for now?" Paradise felt she had perhaps shared too much.

"I do understand, believe it or not. I thought Sydney looked sad, frightened, and trying hard to keep a smile on her face all the while keeping an eye on the door. Clearly she wanted to make a fast exit, maybe even without talking to either of you. I reminded myself that if I only had dead people to whisper to all day, I would be sad, too, but she does it for a living, so I wondered if it was personal... and sure enough." Hope was proud of her adult response to her mom. "Can I help you pack?"

"Hope, that would be wonderful. I need to speak with your father for a second but everything I need is laid out on our bed. I am only taking the backpack on the floor beside the bed, so you can just dump everything into it if you want. It's a short trip."

"Just call me The Ghost Whisperer, mom. Or how about The Morgue Whisperer, or Whispering for the Dead? I'm using the term 'whisperer' because when I talked with Sydney she very clearly told me that I would need to leave my 'outside voice' at home. She also said, 'You do know how to whisper, Hope, right?' She was laughing when she said it, but I could tell it was no joke."

Hope was taking the stairs two at a time when Paradise turned to Thomas. "You wanted to discuss this, my love? I could see it in your eyes and in how your body tightened as I spoke with Hope. Surely you're not suggesting she come with me?"

"If it would put some distance between Hope and Ben, I would suggest she go with you. You could arrange things with Sydney before you leave here, Hope could pack a bag, too, because it would be a long day. You could drive her into the city and Sydney's offices and turn her over to one of Sydney's team members, then drive back out of the city to Sydney's. Lots of driving for you, Paradise. What do you think?"

Without a word, Paradise picked up her phone and pressed a number. Thomas was certain she was calling Sydney, so he gave her some privacy and went upstairs to check on his son and to suggest that Hope not pack her mother's bag just yet.

This time, it was Paradise taking the steps two at a time. "Hope, we have a change of plans. Pack your overnight bag and I'll pack mine. Sydney will meet us in her office because she wants to personally 'turn you over', to quote her, to her best man in the morgue."

Thomas understood without saying a word. He gave Paradise a thumbs-up sign and returned to his coffee downstairs. Lee was still sleeping soundly.

"You wanted to go to the morgue and I believe you wanted to go today. Did I misunderstand? The morgue man might be waiting to meet you." Paradise knew what was coming next.

"I had plans with Ben today, but this is a lot more interesting, so let's pack up. Thanks, Mom."

Hope turned to leave her parents bedroom but stopped in the doorway. "What about your meeting?"

"All settled," Paradise was beginning to pack so Hope knew she had to get busy herself. She would ask more once they were in the car and on the road.

10: A Cape car rental

The girls were in the car and off to Halifax in record time. For some reason, Hope had been unable to reach Ben before they left. Ben being unavailable to her had not happened before in their short relationship. He was always easy to reach. Until this morning...

"Mom, if I don't stay more than a minute or two, could we stop at Ben's so I can explain in person why I can't see him later today? He will understand, but he will worry if I go 'phone-silent', as he calls it, when he is trying to reach me."

Thinking about this, Hope went on. "You know, mother, Ben has not dropped in or called me in a few days and I am just now reflecting on that little detail. I've been busy, too, as you know, but if nothing more, we talk on the phone every day. Sometimes, we talk more than once a day. Or, we used to. Maybe the relationship is over and I just didn't realize it."

Seeing the second car parked beside Ben's car at #8, Paradise was unsure how to handle this. "Hope, honey, there is a second car in Ben's yard, so maybe you should call him later in the day or this evening, rather than barge in on him when he specifically has not taken your calls."

Paradise parked on the side of the road just out of view from Ben's window. She would pull up in front of his home if that's what Hope wanted, or she could make a U turn and use the other end of Cape St Mary Road just as easily. Paradise did not want her daughter to be disappointed by what she might see inside, but at the same time it might ruin her road trip if Ben continued to ignore her calls.

"Ah, that's why he's not answering his phone. He has company. I wonder who it is. Mom, have you seen anyone with Ben? It must be a guy helping him clean the place out so he can continue his renovations. I know he's finished another room so needs to clear junk out of his next path through his home. Sure, pull up and I will run in. He won't mind."

Hope was out of the car before Paradise came to a full stop. Paradise hoped the element of surprise didn't smack her girl upside the head.

She got out of the car just in case Hope needed her, or in case she heard raised voices coming from inside. Call it mother's intuition...Paradise had a bad feeling about this.

Hope didn't hear any noises or any conversation, but the lights were on so she opened the door and stuck her head in as she has always done. "Are you decent?"

"Hope, I'll be right with you. Give me a second to get some clothes on."

Turning to his house guest, Ben whispered, "How fast can you get dressed? Or at the very least cover up? Do you not have a housecoat with you?" Ben was frantic.

Throwing her long, lush hair to one side Danielle was not frantic at all. "Honey, how do I look in your shirt?"

Hope heard it all. She stepped inside and, after a glance at Ben, who was just zipping up his jeans, Hope turned her attention to the tall, skinny and beautiful girl pulling Ben's shirt over her head. "Hi, I'm Hope. Ben's girlfriend."

"That makes two of us honey. I'm Danielle and I just flew in from Paris, so pardon me if I am not yet fully awake. Jet lag is a bitch."

In her mind but not out loud Hope replied with, 'No, you're the bitch.' Her mother would ground her for a lifetime if she said that, so she said nothing for a second or two.

These two have foul mouths, thought Hope for a nanosecond. Her mother would have said, 'language,' followed by another 'language' first to her boyfriend and then to Danielle.

Turning to Ben, Hope asked, in a surprisingly mature voice, "Ben, you are the one person who can clear this up. From my view it seems like Danielle is your girlfriend. Am I wrong?"

Hope turned away so he would not see the tears fall from her face.

Paradise was now at the door and, having heard every word, she hesitated to enter since Hope seemed to be in control. She knew Hope had caught a glimpse of her as she turned to wipe her tears. She gave her mother 'the hand', meaning 'I've got this', so Paradise stepped aside just out of view. Not out of hearing range though.

"Hope, I know you tried to call me. Is everything okay? Is it possible that I could pick you up later today for an hour or two? This is not what it looks like and I would like the chance to explain, in private. Danielle is a friend of mine from Paris. Our families go way back."

"Hey there, cowboy, she might be a kid, but Hope isn't stupid, so tell her the truth or I will."

Just like that Danielle turned ugly on Ben. "Does she know we're engaged, my love?"

"Shut up, Danielle. We were never a couple so there was never a need to break up. You know this."

"In your dreams, my man, if we broke up, I wasn't there for the discussion. Ben, you loved me so sweetly one day. Gave me your mother's engagement ring the next day and asked me to explore the world with you. Where was the 'break up' in all of that?"

Danielle could see she was hurting Hope more than Ben, so she shut up.

"Christ, where did you get my mother's engagement ring? Did

you know I have the local police looking for that ring? Did you take it, steal it, after my parents' funeral when everyone was back at our place for a drink or two?"

Ben was yelling at Danielle. He could yell after Hope left so she was unsure what his goal to his shouting would be.

Ben turned to Hope and spoke in a quiet, earnest tone. "Hope, what she says is not true, and this is why I want to explain things to you in private. In private."

Hope tried to not stumble over her words. "I stopped to tell you mom and I are off to Halifax for a few days. I'm going to be spending some time in a morgue. Get your act together if you want to be my boyfriend."

Turning to Danielle, she said, "I'm sorry if I sound like a bitch, too, but if you are Ben's girlfriend, please know I was 100% unaware of this. I would never have even kissed him once if I knew he was engaged to a woman who now wears his mother's ring. That's pretty significant."

She turned to Ben, again with tears in her eyes, "Ben, how could you do this to me?"

She wanted to make a fast exit. Hope knew if this was a love match, it did not include her. She stopped at the door to think for a second, and got a solid 'thumbs up' from her mother. Hope summed up courage to turn and offer a parting thought with one foot out of the door.

"Ben, while it feels like my heart is shattered in a million pieces, for now I do not have a boyfriend, meaning you only have one girlfriend to worry about. That should lighten your load for a day or two. I honestly don't want to see you or hear from you while my mom and I are in the city."

Stepping outside of the little cottage she had come to love, Hope turned to her mom. "Mother, start the car. Start the car."

11: Windshield time

Paradise wanted to let her girl start the conversation, but it had been almost three quarters of an hour already. The silence was deafening, but she knew Hope was deep in thought, so she kept on driving.

Hope really thought Ben loved her and she was certain she loved him. At the moment, that didn't make her feel a damn bit better. She kept that to herself so she wouldn't have to hear her mother's 'language' reprimand. She was not in the mood for a light-hearted jab.

Finally, Paradise heard a very big sigh from Hope, so she knew a discussion wasn't far off. She was right.

Just before an entire hour of silence...."I didn't think of Ben being a cheater, mom, because I asked him during our first dance if he had a girlfriend and he said, 'no.' That was good enough for me at the time, but now I'm not sure of anything. What do you think, mom?"

"First off all, Hope, remember that your mother spent five years in a Catholic convent. I was there from ages sixteen to twenty-one, so you're thinking about your not-so-faithful boyfriend through the eyes of a sixteen year-old who is far worldlier than I was at your age. My worries at sixteen included trying to find a way to get out of the unflattering black penguin costume I was forced to wear as a wanna-be nun."

"Mom, that's not fair. You're always telling me not to compare my life with your life at my age because the world and everything in it has changed so much."

"Absolutely right. First admission is that I wanted to reach into that mess of a home and smack the lovely and beautiful Ben upside the head. But then I stopped to think, Hope. Ben is a smart man. If he had anything this big to hide (a girlfriend, to be specific) do you think her car would be parked right outside? He had to know you would see it."

"Yes, he would know I might see Danielle's car, but maybe that's what he wanted to have happen. Easy way out of our relationship, because he had to know I would break up with him on the spot."

"Hope, you don't regret saying something, do you?"

Paradise reluctantly stopped talking. This was her young and beautiful daughter's maze to solve and she didn't need her mother making decisions for her.

Some time passed before Hope spoke again. "Change of subject because I think we're getting close to Halifax, right, mom?"

"Honey, we are just halfway to Halifax, should we stop for lunch or a snack and a drink somewhere soon?"

"Sure." Hope knew that would let her mom smile. Hope was smiling too. "I'm on my way to see dead bodies. That will make me stop thinking about anything, including Ben. I will need to focus because I want to remember every second of this trip."

"I don't want to burst your bubble, Hope, but I'm almost certain that you will not see dead bodies today. I'm sure Doctor Scott will want all of my time to be with her in private. She would want to be the one to take you to the morgue, and she wouldn't be able to do that today."

"Tomorrow, then?"

"I don't think so, Hope, but maybe I'm wrong. Lord knows, I've been wrong before. I was surprised Doctor Scott agreed to have you in her upstairs office. The morgue is downstairs and she considers it to be her *main* office. Everything that takes place in the morgue is her responsibility and, believe me, she takes it all very seriously."

"Okay, but, mom...I'm thinking you're wrong. I'll leave it at that for now. Ben has crept back into my head so I'll likely be quiet for a bit. Don't go anywhere, I'll be right back."

Paradise loved the humour in her girl's voice so she didn't say a word...just kept driving.

After forty minutes of deafening silence, Paradise wasn't sure if her girl was sleeping or still deep in thoughts about Ben and her feelings for him. Not to mention what she witnessed before they even got off Cape St Mary Road.

Using a soft voice, she said, "Hope, if you're awake, I am starving and I need a bathroom break. Is that going to be okay with you or would you rather wait in the car and I can find us a lunch to go? I don't want to rush you on any front."

"I don't even know what that last sentence means, mom, but you had me at 'starving' and again at 'bathroom', so let's find a greasy-spoon. I think I have Ben figured out, so I can run it all past you with a mouth full of lunch. I want to have this out of my head when we meet Doctor Scott. And I assume we are calling her 'Doctor' because this is kind of a business call. Correct?"

"You're right, Hope. When I have a business meeting at any time during the day I allow that event to be in my head all day along with everything else churning around in my brain. It's like preparing in advance for everything I will and must deal with on any given day. And when the think-tank is empty...sorry, Hope, I didn't mean to introduce a teachable moment today."

"Well, thank you for that. My brain is so full I can't learn anything else, which is why I need to unload my thoughts about Ben so I have room to turn into a PI in the morgue."

"Roger that," Paradise said with a smile as the exit ramp for Kentville appeared just ahead.

Hope was familiar with the exit. “Forget my idea of finding a greasy spoon. Café Central coming right up. Does Linda know we’re coming?”

12: ben (small b)

"Mac 'n' Cheese is the special today. How lucky are we?"

"Oh, we are lucky *and* special. Get organized, Hope. Load your tray, move along and Linda will cash you out. Linda owns the place, but she also does it all. If I remember correctly, she includes herself when she plans each week's schedule for her staff."

Paradise knew Hope didn't eat out that often because their dinner at home was a 'command performance,' as Hope would call it. Plus, she took her lunch to school, so no line-up for her there. Without her saying much, this was a tiny teachable moment.

Linda saw Paradise and Hope sliding their trays along and the lunch crowd was thinning out so she would have a few minutes to talk. "Hope, my goodness, look at you...all grown up. Sixteen or seventeen? Boyfriend?"

"Hi Linda. I'm sixteen." Hope had a big grin on her face. "Hey, my mom told me you have boys but no girls, Linda. Could you sit with us while we have lunch? Maybe you can help me figure out why my boyfriend is a freaking jerk. He was the perfect boyfriend until this morning."

Paradise wasn't happy to hear Hope share her heartache with Linda, as well as everyone else still in the Café. She was definitely not using her inside voice. "Hope, honey, tone it down a bit. Linda will join us if she can, but only you can solve your problem. If Linda joins us she will be on a break and that means having a bit of 'down time' that we will be invading. Let's 'visit' with her a bit before we introduce, what did you call him, ‘your freaking jerk of a boyfriend.”

Linda got some mac n’ cheese for herself and joined their table almost immediately.

13: all-ben-all-the-time

Linda jumped in almost before she reached the table. "Let's talk while we eat, because I know you're in a rush. I know this because you're always in a rush, Paradise."

"Hey, I thought this was about my daughter and Ben. I'm unsure what to call Ben at the moment. Before we start on Ben, let's at least visit with Linda for a few minutes, Hope."

"Sure." Hope was distracted anyway and didn't mind having a few minutes to herself while her mom and Linda got all caught up.

In line, right in front of their table, Hope observed seven people. All different than the visual she might find at their little café in the Cape.

First up was a lovely-looking policeman. She knew this because the word, all in upper case, was POLICE on the back of what could be a bulletproof vest. She would ask her mom what a bulletproof vest looked like and why it would be needed for a trip to Café Central. Hope wondered for a second if it might be a fake police vest. Her mom would know that, too.

Second in line was a man who clearly thought he was better than those around him. He carried his credit card between his teeth so he could keep his head low and speak to no one while he furiously wrote something down in his little black book. Hope wanted to observe him at the cash to see how he would hand the cashier the credit card presently half in his mouth. Seemed a bit rude, but she would keep that to herself because her mother would call that being judgmental.

Numbers three and four were together, although they had not spoken a word to anyone, including each other. Hope knew they were together because he couldn't keep his hands out of her long hair. It didn't seem to bother her.

Keeping to herself for a bit longer, Hope wondered if she would like her boyfriend to run his fingers through her hair, *if* she had a boyfriend. "I may never find out," Hope said to herself in the same second that she could hear her mother talking to her.

"Earth to Hope, where are you right now?" Paradise was laughing at how long her daughter had ignored her.

"Mom, I've got a few new characters for the mini novel I'm writing in school. I'm ready when you are."

Hope took one more look at the lineup. Most were already through cash and some had picked up their order and were eating, oblivious to the silent interrogation they were being put through in the imagination of young Hope.

Her eyes landed on the one in particular she was looking for. She assumed he was a construction worker because of the tools practically all around his belt, his bright vest and blue, decalled hardhat. He appeared to be very old, maybe over 70, and that made Hope wonder why he wasn't retired already. She was sad for the mysterious man whose image would stay with her until she had him on paper, in her novel.

Hope clapped her hands. "Okay, the rest of this meeting of three is to interrogate one Ben Champagne even though he is not present. Linda, trust me, he's busy with his '*fiancé just in from Paris*', and she's a doll. A tall, beautiful, skinny and obviously wealthy doll."

Just to show her mom that she was not upset at the moment, Hope took a chance and added, "And she's a *bitch*, too, Linda. My mother saw it, too."

"An interrogation is meant to be factual with no judging of the culprit in our headlights," Paradise said. "But, for the first time in my life, and for this one specific case, Hope, I would agree with you. Danielle is a bitch. The way she spoke to you was cruel and insensitive and as your mother, and only for a nanosecond I wanted to scratch her eyes out."

Mother and daughter high-fived each other and even included Linda, who hadn't said much. She hadn't been given the chance.

"I'm sorry, ladies. I have to ask the obvious...who is Ben and why isn't he in Paris with the 'b' right now?" Linda kept one eye on the café and hoped her young guest understood that she was at her work place and had staff to assist if necessary.

"Ben was watching me at mom and dad's wedding party so I asked him to dance. He liked me and I liked him. He just inherited #8 Cape St Mary Road, very close to us. We spent a lot of time together, in spite of my dad's concern, right, mom?"

"Sweetheart, get to the bottom line because we need time for Linda's questions and her advice before we get back on the road. Remember, we cannot keep Doctor Scott waiting."

This time it was Linda who interrupted. "A doctor in the city is likely a specialist. I hope there is nothing wrong, ladies?"

Paradise knew Hope would love to speak up so she gave her the nod to do so.

"Oh. My. God. Linda, Doctor Sydney Scott works in the basement of a building somewhere in downtown Halifax where she keeps dead people twenty-four hours a day. And she's going to make one of her 'people' take me to the basement to show me a dead person or maybe two. I can hardly wait."

Paradise continued, "Linda, Doctor Scott is the Chief Medical Examiner for Nova Scotia. The morgue is in the basement of the building where she works. Hope is fascinated by all of this and is going to spend time with someone on staff both in the offices and the morgue. I have a meeting with Doctor Scott."

"So…back to me," Hope said with a smile.

With a little prompting from her mom, she laid out what had happened and what they had seen when they stopped at Ben's house that morning.

"We might need a part two," said Linda, noticing that Paradise had checked her watch twice. "I have to relieve one of the girls soon, so I'll tell you what I told each of my three boys when they asked for my advice concerning their about-to-be breakup:

1. Break up in person and in private.
2. Be totally honest, even if it's difficult for both of you.
3. Look her in the eye, because she will see you as a former 'shady boyfriend' if you are looking everywhere but at her.
4. Never, under any circumstances, break up over the phone.
5. Unless, I guess, if the boy is in Cape St Mary and the girl is in Paris! And I don't know what the breakup rule is in that case. #1 above probably applies don't you think? Ben should have ensured this breakup was crystal clear before he left town and he should have asked for his mother's ring back, too.
6. Don't tell others you are breaking up with your current girlfriend before you tell her. This could go very badly for you. I watched this happen to one of my boys and it was not pretty."

14: A life in peril

Thomas didn't need to put his PI hat on to determine where Paradise and Hope would be having lunch.

Someone answered on the first ring. "Café Central, may I take your order?"

After confirming his wife and daughter were sitting off to the side with Linda, he asked if he could speak with Paradise.

"May I have your name, sir?"

"Of course, it's Thomas, I am her husband."

"Thomas, is everything okay at home? Strange to have you track me down here."

"My love, everything is okay here, but not so in Lenny's world," Thomas replied. "His partner, Bonde, just called to let you know Lenny is not well. In fact, Paradise, Lenny is dying and he would like to see you. I think you should go to him today. Bonde wasn't even sure Lenny would last for the next twenty four hours."

"I don't know where to start. I have this meeting with Sydney today. Hope has her heart set on time in the morgue. We have a room booked in Halifax. I would like to be there for Lenny, but I have so many commitments here."

Paradise paused long enough for Thomas to jump back into the conversation. "How does this sound? And be honest. I will call Sydney. She will understand. I will cancel your hotel room. Hope will understand and I think you should take her with you, even if it's just company for you, my love. She has friends in Honolulu, and she likes Lenny. Once you see for yourself how he is, perhaps you could take her to see him. All that can be worked out. Just say the word and, by the time you arrive at the airport, your tickets will be waiting for you. I'll check available hotels. If there is anything I haven't thought of, I know you will tell me. That didn't come out the way it was intended," Thomas said, trying to lighten the moment.

"Thank you for understanding how my mind works, Thomas, and thanks for the offer to make all the arrangements for Hope and me. I agree she should come with me. I will let you decide if we should have an open-ended-return ticket and how long you think we might be away, given your call from Bonde. When we arrive at the airport I would like to call and let Lenny know we are coming to him as soon as is humanly possible. I could place a third party call and bill it to our home line."

"Those are only details, honey. Right now you and I have work to do, so we need to get off the phone and get you to the airport. Call Lenny and then call me and I will have more info for you. Drive safe. Love you. Now move..."

Paradise returned to the table while checking her purse for their passports. She carried them in her purse all the time, yet she always checked to ensure they are where they should be. They were.

"First of all, Linda, I am so sorry I tied your phone line up for so long. I should have asked if you have a second line I should be using, but that's water under the bridge now."

Turning to Hope, Paradise took her hand as she spoke quietly, "Change of plans. You and I are going to the airport and flying to Honolulu today. Lenny is very ill and may be dying. He has asked to see us and your dad is making our flight and hotel arrangements while we get ourselves to the airport."

"Should I leave you?" Linda said. "You can stay as long as you need and use our phone again if necessary. I'm going to head to the kitchen and pack some supper for both of you. It will be something you can easily eat on or off the plane. I will be very fast."

She was off in a blur. Paradise was grateful for her friend.

"Hope, we should both go to the washroom before we head out. And I need you to help me settle down a bit before getting behind the wheel. Can you do that?" Paradise had realized she was shaking.

"Sure." Hope said. "I'll go to the bathroom first, okay? And thanks for taking me with you. I hope you're not wishing you had left me in the Cape."

Hope reached over to hug her mother.

"I will love having you along for the trip. I do hope you don't get to see your first deceased person in the form of Lenny, but we need to face facts, Hope. This might be our reality when we arrive. Once we get to the airport and are waiting for our flight I am going to call Bonde and Lenny. You can listen in on everything, if you would like to do that."

"Sure," Hope said over her shoulder en route to the staff bathroom. Linda had told her they could use it anytime they stopped in.

Like the food genie, Linda appeared with a bulging package.

"Thank you for doing this for us, Linda. How much do I owe you?"

"You owe me absolutely nothing, my friend. Drive safely and let me know how things are going when you can. If you can't, you know I will understand. I also know you will be here for lunch during one of your trips to the city."

Hope came flying out of the washroom, almost knocking over a staff member with meals and drinks in both hands, on her way to her customer's table.

"Oh God, I am so sorry," Hope offered as a rather weak apology.

Arriving at the table, Hope scooped up the package. "Mom, I'll take this. Thank you, Linda. I'll be in the car, Mom."

"Sure." Paradise hoped using her daughter's favourite word would bring a smile to her face. And it did.

A quick trip to the washroom, and a moment to hug Linda and thank her once more, and mother and daughter were off.

15: Flight for Lenny

"We can thank your dad for these digs, Hope. The first class lounge is a home away from home. At least, it is for us for these hours before we board our long flight to Honolulu."

Paradise held up her cell phone. "Thomas suggested we return the call from Lenny and Bonde once we are settled in the lounge. He even arranged for us to have this private room for our call, so here goes."

Paradise put the call on speaker and they sat close together to keep voices down.

Paradise recognized Lenny's voice even though it was barely a whisper. "Paradise is that you?"

"Lenny, talk to me. What is going on with you? How ill are you really? I hope this isn't another one of your—"

A female voice interrupted. "Make no mistake, this isn't 'just another one of' anything that you may be thinking and forgive me for interrupting. My name is Bonde, and I would like to continue if I may."

"Of course, and, seriously, thank you for the smack upside the head. The floor is all yours." Paradise mimed smacking herself upside the head since Hope was asking what she meant by the strange expression.

"It was Lenny's cancer that smacked us upside the head, Paradise. He has stage four cancer and he has it in so many parts of his body I could say, 'everywhere' when people ask where it is and it wouldn't be much of an exaggeration. Lenny is asking for the phone so I am going to take his oxygen mask off for a minute or two and hold the phone to his ear."

Paradise could feel the love and gentle manner Bonde was using with Lenny. She started to cry as she heard him try to speak In a small raspy whisper.

"Should have told you about this earlier and asked you to come. I thought I was meaner and tougher than cancer. Not so. Please come. Please hurry, Paradise."

They could hear Bonde talking with Lenny as she gently helped him lie down so she could put his oxygen mask back on.

"For some reason Lenny doesn't like to be sitting up when he has his mask on. He has already nodded off, Paradise. I hope you will come as soon as you can."

"We are waiting to board our plane. We will fly through the night. I will rent a car at the airport and you'll know I've arrived when I knock on your door."

"Okay. Call again if need be. Please hurry, we will be listening for your knock on our door. Lenny will be so happy to hear this wonderful news when he wakes up."

With that Bonde ended the call.

When their flight was called they were quick to line up...*it seems there is no line-up for first class*, Paradise thought. They had no luggage beyond a single backpack for both mother and daughter, so they were quickly on the plane.

Paradise and Hope were all smiles when the captain stopped by to greet them. Captain Doreen Foss and her family owned a cottage beside Paradise's home in the Cape. Hope often looked after the twins. They loved her and she loved them right back.

Captain Foss had been at Paradise and Thomas's wedding not much more than a week ago. "Paradise I have a plane to fly and you and your beautiful daughter have these wonderful seats to sit in for the next eleven hours. Beautiful wedding by the way...I bet you're flying with confetti in your hair."

Captain Foss excused herself for a moment as someone from her staff had a question for her.

"Honestly, you both looked stunning: beautiful, sexy, smart and happy! And there was no question who was in charge of the wedding reception. Hope, I thought your clip-board was a great addition to your ensemble. And it obviously helped you keep the evening rolling smoothly, right up until that last dance. You definitely didn't have it in your hands when you wrapped your arms around that beautiful stranger, though."

Reading through the flight details Paradise saw that a car rental, and a hotel right on the strip (Hope would be thrilled) had been part of the final booking. "My brand-new husband thought of everything."

Picking up on the light mood, Hope punched her mom in the arm and said, "That's my father you're talking about."

16: Bonde steps aside

The knock was quick, personal and impatient. Bonde opened the door prior to knock number three because she wanted to let Lenny sleep for a few more minutes. He slept all the time now, yet he didn't really sleep at all. Cancer and cancer drugs had robbed her lovey Lenny from any form of a relaxing sleep.

"Paradise, I assume? And you must be, Hope? Lenny cried when he heard you were your mom's plus one for the trip." Bonde offered hugs all around.

"Bonde, thank you for your gracious welcome. How is the patient this morning?"

Paradise was nervous and wanted to ask if Lenny was still alive but decided against it. She was confident everything would become clear within the next few minutes.

"Where should I begin? Lenny was up most of the night with excitement. There isn't always a lot of excitement for a palliative man to look forward to. He wanted to have his shower at 5 am, so that's what we did. He knew he would need a long nap after a hot shower. Next, he fussed over what clothes to wear and changed his mind a number of times. Now, I'm going to go and make sure he is ready for his guests. After you both greet him, Hope, maybe you could step out of the room with me. Lenny doesn't hear well where there is more than one voice speaking at a time. Finally, take a bit of advice from someone who has made the mistake a million times. Do not tell Lenny that he *looks good*. If you do he won't believe a word you say following the 'lie', as he calls it. He knows it's hard to know what to say, so say that. So, you two sit and relax. Lenny will tell me if he is able to come to the living room or if I'm to bring you to him. I will leave you when I feel Lenny is comfortable...not a moment before."

Bonde smiled as she walked down the hallway to their bedroom, and heard Hope say, "She is a bad-ass and I like her, mom."

"I agree. Bonde is all that. And I think she is very good for Lenny. That's all we care about right now."

Paradise was tearing up, so decided to take a moment to think only good thoughts about Lenny. She knew Hope was doing the same thing. Hope always saw the good in people.

Within minutes Bonde was back. "Come quickly, Lenny is slipping away. He can't get out of bed but at least he's dressed and lying on top of the quilts. We take that as a win."

Bonde walked back into their room with Paradise and Hope just behind her.

"My love, look who has come to visit with us. It's Paradise and Hope."

Lenny was propped up with pillows so he was sitting at eye level with everyone.

"And I have warned them not to tell you that you look good today," Bonde said with a chuckle.

They had agreed Hope would approach Lenny first and say whatever she carried in her heart. Then she and Bonde would leave the room to give Lenny and Paradise a bit of alone time.

"Lenny, my friend, you look like Hell." Leave it to Hope to break the ice with an off-colour line. "Seriously, though, we were very sad flying over to see you. Cancer is no joke, eh?"

Leaning in Hope gave Lenny a hug and whispered in his ear, "I love you, Lenny, and so does my mom. My dad, not so much."

Lenny hugged Hope as well but he couldn't speak. He could only cry.

"These are happy tears, Hope," Bonde said. "Lenny is so appreciative of you coming with your mom. Let's you and I find something to watch on television." Turning to Lenny, she said, "My love, I am going to let you have some private time with Paradise. If you need me for anything, ask Paradise to come and get me."

Paradise left her chair and sat on the bed beside Lenny. She wanted to touch him and feel close to him as they spoke. She could see that Lenny wanted to say something, so she sat silently, holding his hand.

Finally, he called up the courage. "Paradise, when I heard you were flying here, I felt special. You always found ways to make me feel special. You saw intelligence in me that others did not. You gave me strength, courage and love even though you refused to call it that."

With that Lenny closed his eyes, and added, "I'm not dead, by the way. I am just going to close my eyes and catch my breath. You always could be exhausting, you know." He opened his eyes and they enjoyed a warm smile before it was Paradise's turn to speak.

"During our flight, Hope and I talked about you. We said 'positive thoughts only', but that was the only rule. We could have talked the entire time. Lenny, I will forever remember you as someone who saw me as his equal, treated me like a woman, shared everything you had, told me your deepest secrets and trusted me with your darkest sins. I am forever grateful to have you in my life. All positive thoughts, I promise."

"Would you mind getting Bonde for me? I have to live with her after you leave and I don't want her to feel that we have pushed her out into the cold."

Lenny closed his eyes and Paradise worried that he would be dead in minutes. She hurried to find Bonde.

"Bonde, Lenny is asking for you. He loves you and doesn't want you to feel he and I pushed you away. His words not mine. I think that speaks to his love for you. Now get in there."

Bonde left the room quickly and Paradise turned to her daughter. "I think we got here just in time, Hope. I don't think Lenny will last another day. He doesn't seem to be in pain, so I'm sure he's on pretty strong medication. I am so glad they called us and I am so glad my husband suggested that you come with me. I will need someone to stroll along the strip with me after we check into our hotel on Kalikawa Avenue. Shades on, even if there is no sun. Tears allowed...now and when we are on the beach. You okay, sweetheart?" Paradise knew she was fighting the inevitable.

"I guess I am." Hope was searching for words. "I know it's about Lenny, not about us having fun. But, mom, thanks for the location of our hotel and for mentioning a walk along the beach. I wanted to ask if we could go to the beach as soon as we check in, but I'm trying to think like an adult and understand how you must be feeling right now."

"Don't rush thinking like an adult, Hope. That will come all too soon believe me. For now, for this trip in particular, you have my permission to act like a sixteen-year-old. Like an immature sixteen-year-old, if you feel the need," Paradise said with a smile, before adding, "You can even talk about Ben, if you like."

"Ben who?"

Mother and daughter shared a lighter moment that was broken when Bonde rushed into the room, tears covering her face and t-shirt. "Oh my God, I need a hug, girls."

Paradise and Hope both reached out to Bonde as they engulfed her with arms everywhere.

Hope was on edge. "Why don't I go and sit with Lenny, if that's okay, Bonde? You and my mom can talk for a few minutes if you need a break." Bonde's body language was frightening Hope.

"Is Lenny sleeping?" interrupted Paradise, who was also on

edge. She recognized it in her daughter's voice so wanted to take some of the load off of her shoulders. "What do you think we should do, Bonde?"

As Paradise spoke the words she saw everything in Bonde's eyes. She turned to look at Hope and gathered her in her arms before speaking, almost in silence because she knew the answer to her question.

"Bonde," Paradise whispered. "Is Lenny gone?"

"What are you saying?" Hope spoke as she bolted down the hall to Lenny's room. She knew he was too ill to get very far. "Wherever you've gone, Lenny, I will help you. We need to get your ass back here in bed. Don't tell mom I swore."

As she opened the bedroom door Hope understood what Bonde had been telling her and her mom...mostly she had been talking with Paradise. Bonde's words were ringing in Hope's ears as she looked at Lenny. He looked dead.

Hope took Lenny's hand. He was dead.

She silently asked God to wrap his arms around Lenny as soon as he arrived in Heaven. Her sixteen-year-old self matured in a second.

Needing her mother, Hope bolted the other way when she entered the hallway. She needed her mother's arms around her.

Suddenly, moving to the bright lights of downtown Honolulu didn't excite mother *or* daughter. Their eyes reached each other as Bonde asked if they would mind bunking in with her for a day or two.

With one voice they replied, "Absolutely, anything you need."

Three ladies hugged each other once more as they shared their tears and felt love for each other.

Paradise, always the list-maker, told Bonde she didn't want to begin with, 'Have Lenny removed from the house."

"I've got this," said Bonde. "Lenny and I talked about his death at length, and again when his palliative care doctor told us it could be any day. My God, that was only a few days ago."

Bonde seemed to need a minute so Hope and Paradise sat quietly holding her hands.

"Paradise, he waited for you. He assumed you were going to call him from your home in Nova Scotia. I didn't want to tell him you were both en route because, with the airlines, anything can go wrong."

Paradise wrote her list and assigned every item to one of the three of them and asked Bonde if she had missed anything.

Bonde went to prepare Lenny for his departure via the hearse that Jalen had booked and paid for several days ago when they began to worry that he would die quickly. His body would be taken to the crematorium and his ashes would be ready for pick up in 'about a week.'

It had all seemed so cold to both Lenny and Bonde. "It was important to Lenny that he make that final payment himself. Jalen left to go and make the payment for Lenny and me, but of course he took it out of his own account. Jalen shared that with me just before you arrived. He was here very early this morning. He knew that Lenny was stronger in the morning and he always liked having Jalen 'drop in.'"

Hope retrieved their luggage from the car rental.

Paradise called Thomas to fill him in.

"Don't cancel the hotel room just yet, sweetheart," he said. "You might find that you and our girl need a few days on your own before heading to the airport."

"Thank you, Thomas. I'll fill in the blanks when we get back home. At the moment this is a lot to take in...for Hope as well as myself."

17: Halekulani Hotel on Kalakowa Avenue

Paradise and Hope tried in vain to be excited as they explored their upgraded hotel suite, compliments of Lieutenant Commander Jalen Lexis of Hawaii 2.0.

Lenny had been in the witness protection program, working and living within the walls of 2.0, when Paradise first met him. They worked the night shift together. Thomas was not at all pleased with the unilateral decision Paradise had made to take the night shift. He felt the shift would better be covered by two men, not one man and one woman.

Thomas had lost that particular 'discussion' in more ways than he would ever want mentioned. Paradise and Thomas were 'cold' with each other for several days, and that had been a first.

Hope brought Paradise back to the present. "Mom, have you ever been in a suite like this, like ever? I think this is bigger than our house."

Paradise wished Thomas had been able to make the trip with them. Their honeymoon had lasted less than forty-eight hours. She made a mental note to take brochures home to share with Thomas.

"To answer your question, no I have never been in a suite like this." Paradise put her arms around her daughter. "Thank you again, sweetheart, for coming on this heartbreaking trip with me."

"It would have been worse, mom, if you had to call to tell me

Lenny was dead, or if you kept that all bottled up until you got home. To tell us I mean. Being here is what I wanted, I promise. I didn't think he would be dead only minutes after we saw him, though. That was a real downer."

Putting an arm around Hope, Paradise wanted to change the subject but not before giving her daughter the biggest hug ever. "I didn't know he would die that fast either, but I think Lenny might have hung on until you and I arrived to hug him one more time."

"Oh. My. God. Mother is that even a thing? Hanging on to life a bit longer than you might want to just so you could see someone you wouldn't see again?" Hope clearly didn't believe her mother, and she also took her words literally.

Paradise replied, "Daughter-of-mine, as I respond to your latest query let's both change our clothes for a walk down Waikiki Beach. It's too dark for us to be safe going for a swim, but we will be okay on the beach or the boardwalk. You pick."

Clearing her throat, Paradise continued, "We will see Lenny again if we believe in heaven, so let's believe for one thing, Hope, and one more thing: let's be sure there isn't going to be a funeral. I know what Bonde said, but her eyes said something else. In the morning let's call the Lieutenant Commander just to be sure. He'll know what's going on and what Lenny wanted."

"Mom, forgive me if my sixteen-year-old mind is wrong about this, but I saw how Bonde stepped aside to give us time alone with Lenny. I also saw how she seemed to make herself smaller at the same time. Asking you to come must have been rough on her."

Hope was unsure if she should say anything more. She wasn't finished, though, and she couldn't leave anything unsaid. "Mom, think about this, please, and don't be mad at me for saying it. Maybe the funeral is between Lenny, his lady, Bonde, and perhaps the Lieutenant Commander, but no one else. Just think about it, okay? We came for Lenny, not for Bonde."

"Hope, we have had so many wonderful conversations walking along Mavillette Beach back home. We call it our windshield time and I think it was you who brought that expression from the car to the beach, remember? That was a few years ago. Looking straight ahead and not having to look each other in the eye, it's safe to say anything, to ask anything and to cry if you want to. Am I right, was it you?

"It was me, mom. We were driving from the Cape to Halifax one day and it seemed to take forever. That's when our windshield stories were born."

"Hope, thank you for your honesty and for having noticed when Bonde seemed to lose confidence, making her feel small. It won't be late when we get back to the hotel, so let's call Bonde to make sure she is okay and tucked in for the night. We can say, at that time, that we are going to have to return home in the next day or two. I'll ask if we can call her after the funeral so she can tell us about it, if she chooses to share. We will take our lead from her."

As the ladies entered their suite some time later, the phone was ringing. "Can I answer, mom? Just to say hi and bye and then I'll give you the phone."

Paradise nodded, noting that her daughter had already answered the phone.

"Hello?"

"Paradise, is that you?"

"No, this is Hope. It's a bit late. Who is calling, please?"

"Nice manners, young lady. I like that. My name is Jalen and I'm a friend of both of your parents."

"You wouldn't happen to be Jalen as in Lieutenant Commander Jalen Lexis, sir?"

"Yes and no. On my own time, and when I am talking with friends and family, I am simply Jalen. May I speak with your mother, Hope?"

"Sure." Hope was already handing the phone to her mom.

"Jalen, our hotel suite is incredible and we appreciate it so much. What is even more incredible is that in speaking with Bonde I learned both she and Lenny have been paid their full salary to date. That's very generous of you, sir."

"Oh, enough with the 'sir', Paradise, you know me better than that. You're not at the warehouse at the moment."

Paradise thought she heard anger in Jalen's voice but she didn't question him.

"Sorry, Paradise, that must have sounded unkind. I am so upset over Lenny's death I am almost paralyzed. That's a bit of an exaggeration, but not by much. You may not have known this, but Lenny was the son I never had. No excuse to be rude, though."

"Please, Jalen, no need to apologize. I think we all feel somewhat paralyzed by Lenny's death, at least the fact that the end came so suddenly. I could hardly believe it, and poor Hope thought when she heard Bonde say, 'he's gone,' that she meant exactly that. Lenny had left the building. Disappeared. Gone. She ran to look for him... only to find him dead in their bed."

"Is Hope settled a bit now, Paradise?"

"Yes, she's already fast asleep. It's been quite a day for my girl." Paradise wanted to go to bed as well, but she didn't like to be rude to the Lieutenant Commander!

"I'm going to check flights for tomorrow night, Jalen. We love it here but we just want to get back to Cape St Mary and Thomas. And, to be honest, we need to sleep in our own beds."

"Let us arrange that for you, Paradise. Do you want the red eye? That would give you all day tomorrow. I could pick you up late in the afternoon and we could spend a few minutes with Bonde. Then I will drive you to the airport and have you through security in a flash."

"I have a car rental—"

"Already looked after. Say the word and I will have it returned to your rental agency."

"You do think of everything."

Paradise was a bit taken aback by all that Jalen had taken for granted, but, knowing that it probably made him feel useful, she let it go. "You will have to feed us in there somewhere, though, because Hope and I will sleep all through the flight to Toronto and again during our connecting flight to Halifax."

"Let me know if I'm overstepping, but would you like to have an early dinner with Bonde? She hasn't let me in since Lenny died and, while I know how gutted she is, I'm not sure she should be alone at a time like this." Jalen was hopeful she would say yes.

"I would love that, and I know Hope would as well, but can you make sure Bonde is okay with seeing us? Yesterday, I felt strongly that she was anxious to close the door behind us when we left. My God, was it only yesterday?"

She knew she was bone tired, but what Paradise found surprising was that she was swearing!

"Paradise, you have my word. I will tread very lightly with Bonde, especially because it's you and we all know what Lenny thought of you. I happen to know that when Lenny asked her to call you she didn't flinch for a second. She made the call immediately. When Lenny was sleeping, she called me to share that she wasn't sure she could open the door and let you in. She said something about feeling like she was lost, so I interrupted to remind her I don't deal well with feelings…just the facts, please."

Jalen smiled and that smile came through the phone line to Paradise. She felt it.

"Not to make plans for you," she said, "but maybe Bonde would like us to pick up dinner en route to her place. I know some of the foods she liked to eat with Lenny and we could modify that menu a bit to make it a brand-new menu for Bonde."

Paradise couldn't imagine going out to a restaurant for a meal just after losing your partner. "I know we all grieve differently, but —"

"Roger that, Paradise. Unless you hear otherwise, I will pick you up at 1400 hours tomorrow and will share our itinerary with you and Hope en route to Bonde's home."

"Roger that, sir."

Paradise hung up before Jalen had a chance to remind her to call him by name unless they were working in the warehouse.

Hanging up on 'the big boss' gave Paradise a really belly laugh. She couldn't wait to share that little bit of information with Thomas.

Hope had taken the smaller bedroom, leaving the master suite with the incredible view for her mom. Paradise had a long hot shower, even washed her hair, thinking Hope might want to do a bit of shopping after a long beach walk in the morning and this would save a bit of time.

She observed that Hope had washed her long hair as well. They could hit the ground running in the morning.

18: A surprising bond

Bonde walked through her home as if she didn't know she lived there. She saw everything for the first time, and she saw nothing at all.

She placed the call before she could talk herself out of calling the one woman she had always been jealous of. It was not quite five am, so she might be calling a tad too early.

A very young and sleepy voice at the other end of the phone finally spoke. "Hello…before it's time to wake up and you better not have made my mother wake up…she hasn't had much sleep. I haven't, either. Can I assume whoever this is has called the wrong room?"

Hope prayed that wasn't a sob she heard at the other end of the connection.

It was, and Hope was gutted when she recognized the voice. "Hope, honey, please just let me say this, and if you don't ever want to talk to me again I'll understand, but—"

"Oh. My. God. Bonde, I am so sorry. My mother will kill me for answering our phone that way. Especially because it's you. Are you okay? Stupid question, I know. Okay, I'll stop talking now."

"You don't need to apologize to me, Hope. Here's the thing…I haven't slept all night and I know it's early. Jalen called me a few hours ago to say he was picking you and your mom up later today and that he would like to bring you out here to pick me up and we could maybe go to dinner. But I need some 'girlfriend' time and wanted to ask if I could come to your hotel this morning. I have never been in your hotel and it's been years since I have walked along Waikiki Beach with a friend. I thought we could let Jalen know that we are spending the day together but we will be hungry for dinner so he could pick us all up at your hotel." Bonde stopped to take a breath.

Hope took advantage of the silence. "Here's a plan, Bonde. You need a bit of sleep as much as we do. How about you show up around ten am, which gives us almost five more hours to sleep. Then when you arrive here, stop at the restaurant and see if someone can follow you to our suite while they carry a pot of black coffee and a few fresh muffins, charge it to our room, and we can chat while we all get ready for the beach, dinner and, in our case, a plane ride. I'm going to suggest to mom that when we dress this morning we do so knowing we won't be changing until we touch down in Nova Scotia. Now, can I please go back to sleep? For the love of God, it's not even four am, Bonde. I'll clear everything with mom when she wakes up and she will be fine with all of it."

"Thank you, Hope. You have become a serious decision maker. I will send a note to Jalen to share our plans for the day."

"Good night, Bonde."

"Good morning, young lady."

"Hope, what in God's name is going on in the middle of the night? Whom are you talking with?"

"Mom, we have a wake-up call at nine in the morning...only a few hours away. Go back to sleep. Hit the shower as soon as you wake up. I will do the same and then we can sit and talk it all out. Good night!"

"Did you remember to order lots of coffee for 9 am?"

"It will be closer to 10 when it arrives, but it will be worth it. I promise, mom."

Finally, sleep came to mother and daughter.

19: Making room for a third

Hope turned the shower off and grabbed a towel for her hair. Then she stepped into the lush robe that had been waiting for her when she arrived. She thought it might be the most luxurious bathrobe she had even worn. Her mom's en suite had the same robe, just in a different colour.

Suddenly, Hope heard her mother drying her hair already.

"Good God, mother, how did you beat me up? Our alarm hasn't even gone off yet and here we are!"

"Settle down, Hope. It's way too early in the morning to feel you are late for anything. Here, I'll pour you a coffee."

"Coffee? Where did you get this coffee, mother, and did it come with anything else...or with *anyone* else?"

"Hope, what is wrong with you this morning and what are you talking about?"

Accepting the hot coffee, Hope sat on her mom's bed and shared the late-night call from Jalen followed by the call from Bonde. She followed that with their pre-arranged plans for the day. Pre-arranged in that she had made the plans while her mother slept.

"And finally, mom, when Bonde arrives she will call room service from the lobby to place our order and then she will follow breakfast and more coffee up to our suite in less than an hour from now."

Hope was off the bed, pouring herself a second cup and topping her mom's coffee up, while explaining that whatever they wore, they would wear it for the day and night because they should both pack everything else up and fill their backpacks. "We can leave everything with the concierge downstairs. I know you carry a huge purse, mom, so please pack it light, if you can, just in case we make any purchases for when our airplane touches down and we head back to the Cape."

Hope was beyond hyper on this particular morning. "At the very least, we need a 'prize' for Lee. Every gift he receives he refers to it as his 'prize'."

Paradise smiled as she reflected on those she would like to bring a small gift for. There would be no celebration when she and Hope arrived home. This was not the sort of trip that ends in celebration.

Late last night, while Hope was making plans with Jalen, Paradise had been on the phone with Thomas, firming up plans for their arrival back in Halifax. Paradise was sure there was something Thomas wasn't telling her as he explained that Wilmot, Marie and Rescuee were going to drive him to the Halifax airport so he could pick up their car. Thomas would check in to their hotel, so all the small things would be attended to before he drove back to the airport to await their flight.

Paradise had pressed him enough to know there was an urgency to meet with Sydney at her home. She was glad to hear that Thomas had done some digging and that, by the time their plane touched down in Halifax he would, ideally, have a full understanding of what had taken place to force this urgent meeting.

Their plans had already changed since Thomas and Paradise spoke last night. Lee was supposed to make the trip with Thomas and Hope would watch him at the hotel while Paradise and Thomas met with Doctor Scott, but now he would stay home. The coroner had plans in place for Hope to spend the day at her offices, including a secret side trip to the morgue. Thomas and Paradise would leave their hotel only after Doctor Scott's driver had arrived to take Hope downtown.

Sydney had thought of every detail that would make Hope enjoy her time in her public office and in her second office, the morgue.

Denis and Waine had learned that Thomas had a long day or two in the city so they asked if Lee could stay at Cabin #3 with 'the Uncles', as everyone now called them. Lee loved the idea and, truthfully, Thomas did as well.

20: Remembering Lenny

The knock on the door was not unexpected. Both Paradise and Hope opened the door wide to a smiling 'room service' delivery, and when the server stepped inside to leave the array of breakfast goodies, including more coffee, they spotted Bonde lurking behind and not looking at all like the Bonde they had left not twenty-four hours ago. Clearly, she had not changed her clothes, either.

Paradise was proud of her daughter when Hope took charge of the situation. "Hey, Bonde get in here."

Hope reached out and brought Bonde inside with a bear hug that lifted her off of her feet. "I see you brought your 'today' clothes with you. Come on over to my room where you can have a shower or a bath or just clean up. Take your time. Make it about you. It looks like you haven't had a second for yourself in some time. Likely since Lenny moved in with you, I bet."

Hope was on a roll and wasn't finished yet. "Mom and I aren't going anywhere and we are in no rush at all. If Jalen picks us up and we haven't left the room yet, we are both good with that. Fresh towels. You can use my robe and everything you need is in the bathroom. If you need something that you don't see, just rummage around and I bet you will find it."

With a kiss on the cheek, Hope left Bonde standing utterly speechless.

Hope quietly closed the bedroom door and went back to her mom's suite. "Oh. My. God. Mother, not you, too? Why are you crying? What did I miss?"

"Lower your voice, Hope. I couldn't help hearing your every word because you were not using your inside voice. When Bonde returns, let's not comment on how rough she looks, okay? She has been planning a funeral and that's not easy for anyone to go through."

Mother and daughter were dressed almost totally alike, yet they had not intentionally coordinated their outfits. "Look at us. Matchy-matchy, mom. This is pretty funny. White t-shirts under black jackets, and black Capri pants: how cool are we?"

Hope was laughing and her mom hadn't seen many smiles on her daughter's face since they arrived.

Paradise took a leap of faith with her next question. "Hope, how many times has your mind been filled with thoughts of Ben? I thought we could talk about you and Ben for a few minutes before Bonde joins us. Has it been intentional that you have not wanted to talk about him, or are you just not talking about him with me? Either way is fine, I just want you to know that you can discuss anything with me…even boyfriend stuff." Paradise hoped she hadn't miss-stepped.

"Mom, I honestly don't think I want a steady boyfriend. They are a lot of work, you know. I challenge myself, wondering if I'm running away from a problem that I have to deal with when we arrive home, or am I really serious about being 'single' for now. What should I do, mom?"

"That's not a question I can answer for you, sweetheart. However, you're sixteen, so I welcome the opportunity to offer some thoughts I have about you and Ben as a couple."

Clearing her throat to give herself time to think about what she wanted to say, Paradise continued, "I watched you when we stopped at Ben's home and ran smack into his 'girlfriend'. I saw confusion on your face, and why not? Has this seemingly-wonderful boyfriend been lying to all of us? I don't think he has, Hope. I think in his mind, they broke up, but not so in her mind. Since leaving the convent, I have learned that some men, probably most men, simply don't talk about their feelings."

Paradise smiled and suggested they could pick this up once they boarded the night flight to Toronto and before they both nodded off.

Bonde opened the bedroom door and joined Paradise and Hope. "Coffee, please. In the name of God, I need coffee. This will be my first coffee of the day and the day's near half over."

Laughs all around. Both Hope and Paradise understood the need, and the value, of that first cup of coffee.

Paradise spoke first. "Actually, we fly at midnight, so there is more day left than you might have imagined, Bonde."

"Now, this is the Bonde we met a day or two ago," said Hope, as she poured coffee all around. "This is not our first cup of coffee. In fact it's not even our second, so you have some catching up to do."

As tears glistened and dropped onto her cheeks Bonde explained how grateful she was to be able to see Paradise and Hope in a more pleasant surrounding. "Lenny had wanted to give his body to science, so I'm left with nothing tangible of Lenny's at all. When he first received his cancer diagnosis, he gave me a small note with the phone number of the person I was to call when he died. I was still in the 'you're not dead yet so stop rushing this' phase. God, I'm sorry to dump on you both."

Paradise moved to sit directly in front of Bonde. "What time is Jalen picking us up, first of all?"

Bonde had gotten her tears and hiccups under control and she began to relax. "We are to call him anytime, but if he doesn't hear from us, he will be here at 7 pm. Dinner first, and then we will take you to the airport. Jalen lives not far from us, from me, so he can easily drop me off en route home."

21: Bonde

"Do you even know how perfect your idea is, Bonde?" Paradise said. "To make the purchase, pay for everything and have one large package mailed to our home is the best, and the easiest way, to appreciate everyone in and around the Cape. We will be eating macadamia nuts for a year. And the tiny packaging is just the right size for what I have in mind."

Paradise jumped up from the edge of the bed, where she had been sitting since Bonde arrived. "We haven't left the hotel yet and I have purchased everything I need all in one phone call. I can't thank you enough for the suggestion."

Paradise paused to remind herself she might be showing a bit too much excitement while they were all mourning Lenny's death.

Bonde said, "This particular macadamia nut storefront is owned by the closest male friend Lenny had...Lenny felt unsafe around most people during the few times he was outside of the 2.0 offices."

Bonde paused to eat the last bite of her muffin, the last scrap of her breakfast. She washed it down with the last drop of coffee in her cup. "A prepaid order of this size and Buddy will feel like a million dollars, believe me. When I called your order in, he kept asking if I should verify it one more time. And when I said I had your charge card right in front of me, ready to pay, he asked me to marry him. I let him down gently, saying he had already picked the cream of the crop when he found his wife. We were both chuckling when we hung up."

Bonde was so glad she had mentioned the idea of macadamia nuts.

"I hate to break up this 'adult conversation'," Hope said, "but it is now after 2 pm and we are still inside this hotel. Which is lovely, by the way, but I really want a walk on this beautiful beach we can enjoy literally steps from us. Waikiki and all of its splendour is waiting for us."

She began clearing the dishes and putting chairs back where they belonged, hoping her mother and Bonde would leave with her because, one way or the other, she was going to be on that beautiful beach for at least an hour before Jalen picked them up.

"I can help with your luggage, if you want." Bonde wanted to be helpful in any way she could. She was thrilled to be with Lenny's great love, Paradise, and her beautiful daughter. It was easy to see why Lenny would have fallen in love with Paradise. For now, Bonde decided she would keep that to herself. She was having a bit of a 'girl-crush' and that made her feel a bit better about how she was going to get through the day and all of the days to come without Lenny.

"Thanks, but we're good," Paradise said. "We came with these backpacks only and we can leave them with the concierge while we go out for a couple—"

"You've been here for five days, and you have no luggage? I wouldn't count a backpack as luggage!"

Bonde felt light-hearted. She knew being with Paradise for one full day would give her a few positive memories. There hadn't been any of them since Lenny's cancer took him away from her so quickly.

22: Jalen Lexis

"Ladies," Jalen said, "I was watching the three of you with sand between your toes and our Hawaiian breeze rearranging your hair as you walked back toward the hotel. The three of you holding hands! What a beautiful sight for these tired old eyes."

As they walked to Jalen's car, Hope said, "You should know, Lieutenant Commander, or whatever they call you, that when we went to the front desk to pay for our hotel bill, my mother was pissed that you had paid for everything. Are you rich or something?"

"Hope, I'm rich because you have entered my life. I have heard so much about you, and here you are. You are everything Lenny has told me about you, and about beautiful Cape St Mary as well."

Bonde was smiling as she turned to Jalen. "So I'm reprimanded when I use what you call foul language, but when Hope says she's pissed, you just let that go?"

"Bonde, when you joined 2.0, every time you opened your mouth you spewed words that are best left silent. And don't forget, young lady, you will be back working within the walls of 2.0 before too many weeks pass and my rules always apply when in the warehouse. Remember? Understand?"

"Yes, sir!"

During a beautiful dinner, with a full view of the ocean, they toasted and roasted Lenny...always with respect. Paradise and Hope truly hated for the evening to end, but they couldn't let their flight leave without them, so Paradise was on watch-alert all evening.

"It's time, ladies. Bonde will tell you, Hope, and remind you, Paradise, that I do not handle public displays of feelings or emotions very well, so understand this is a good bye that I will find hard to get through. Forgive me if I seem cold once we are at the airport and all out of the car for 'hugs all around.' I detest hugging when both parties feel awkward and say things that they don't mean, like, 'Let's do lunch' or 'I'll give you a call.' Both parties know there will be no lunch and no call."

Bonde jumped in. "Hey, I've got you, sir! Lean on me...*please* lean on me. You know I'm kidding, Jalen, and I'll get you out of this without tears, or at least I will give it my all."

"Thank you, Bonde. I appreciate that."

Only minutes later all four car doors opened and three tearful ladies stepped out in front of the airport terminal. Jalen played it safe and explained where they would go to find their gate. When to turn left and when to turn right. No emotion required.

Taking his arm, Bonde tried her best to keep it light. "Sir, you do know these ladies have flown out of Honolulu before, yes?"

Jalen could nod but that was about it.

The only one who hadn't stepped up to the imaginary microphone was Paradise. It was appropriate that she spoke last. "Jalen, your detailed attention to this trip has been second to none and we thank you so much from the bottom of our hearts. I promise to keep in touch...and I sincerely mean that."

When Paradise took Bonde's hands in hers they were both already crying. "You've become a dear friend within a few hours of our meeting you, Bonde, and all of that was within the most difficult of circumstances. Hope and I are so grateful that you allowed us time with Lenny. And we thank you for taking such good care of him."

Turning to Jalen, Paradise hugged him and whispered, "Keep an eye on her for us and don't be a stranger. We have phones in rural Nova Scotia, you know."

"Off you go, ladies. I've got to get *this* lady home in time for work in the morning. Work for me, I mean, not you, Bonde. We can talk about your return date another day. Maybe you should have someone stay with you for a few days, just to be there when you want to talk about Lenny or simply vent over things, like all of his belongings that you will have to deal with. What do you think? And before you say it...*no*...I am not applying for the job."

"Thank you, Jalen, but what I need is some 'me' time, I think, and being alone will be good for me. You're a good man, Lieutenant Commander Jalen Lexis."

Bonde gave Jalen a brief hug then moved quickly around the car to jump in the passenger seat.

While they were bantering, Hope and Paradise had moved on. They were already out of sight.

Jalen and Bonde were reflecting on exactly how many miles away Mavillette Beach was from Honolulu. It was easy windshield conversation, Bonde thought, but she kept that to herself.

Bonde didn't waste any time jumping out of the car when Jalen pulled up to her front door. She didn't trust herself to not get emotional and start crying again. What she didn't realize was that Jalen felt exactly the same way.

Jalen purposely did *not* get out of his car. He leaned over the passenger seat, looked up at Hope and offered food for thought. "I will leave you alone for a few days, if you promise to call me during the day just to check in."

In a whisper Bonde replied, "I'll try to remember what hours you are normally *out of the office* during the day and I will leave a message at that time. Please *do not* call me back unless I ask you to. I'm serious when I say I need to be alone for a while."

Reaching in and taking Jalen's hand, Bonde went on, "You don't 'do emotion', but believe me that, while I don't normally cry, I can't seem to stop. So for now all I can promise is that I will stay in touch and I will return to work as soon as I possibly can. If you would like to stop paying me as of Lenny's death I can manage financially on my own for a few months, I think. I don't even know whom you hired to replace both Lenny and me."

Jalen knew Bonde was literally all over the map with her thoughts while he had said all he had left in his talk-tank. Removing her hand from his, he put the car in 'drive' and slowly took his foot off the brake. "Bonde, please go inside and get some rest. I hate to leave you like this but I need to have a bit of rest myself. We will talk soon."

Bonde watched him drive slowly away. She realized she didn't even know where he lived. "Drive safe, Jalen. Please drive safe."

Jalen knew he would not sleep. He was too wound up. There was too much grief. He would miss Lenny beyond measure. He had just cried for the first time in many years.

Lenny had shown him what true emotion, true friendship and true love actually look like. Lenny also taught Jalen that life is too short to work every day, all day, and half of the night.

At home, before nodding off, Jalen made a metal note to go through all personal items in what had been Lenny's cubicle at the warehouse. He wouldn't take anything, not a single thing, but he needed to know what Bonde would be facing when she came in to pick up his things.

23: Ben & gone-girl

All Ben could do was wait. Hope would come to him if she wanted to. The visual of him and Danielle might have been more than her sixteen-year-old mind could forgive and forget.

Prior to Danielle leaving and returning to France, Ben had asked Thomas to 'drop in' one day. He knew Thomas would believe him and might, just might, one day convince Hope that he was 'not all bad.'

Just about everyone in the Cape had been by to help Ben with something in the house...floors, ceilings, walls, electrical and basically anything and everything that required attention. One or two of the workmen had met Danielle, and it wasn't long before every single man in the Cape was eager to drop-on-by and ask what they could do to help with the re-build.

The day Thomas was scheduled to drop in, he called Ben to suggest meeting on Mavillette Beach instead, since it was a beautiful day for the beach. He felt if he had to listen to this story sitting in a small room he might kill Ben before their coffee was cold. He also had a few things to say to Ben before meeting Danielle.

Thomas took a day to think Ben's story over before he agreed to speak with Hope. "Look, I'll tell Hope that you are not all bad. I will also tell her a few things about Danielle, but not much. There are always two sides to a story, and this will be an interesting lesson for Hope to learn, bearing in mind that my daughter is sixteen years old and you are, or maybe were, her first boyfriend. Hope told her mother she might be in love with you. That bothered me. It bothered me the day I heard about her feelings for you and it bothers me today."

Thomas decided to bring Wilmot and Marie up to date while they drove him to the Halifax airport to meet Paradise and Hope. It started because, like most people in the Cape, they had heard a very different version of what had been happening at #8 Cape St Mary Road.

Marie gave him the perfect opening to discuss all of this mess."Is it true that Ben is married to someone from Paris and that she has now moved into our little community? I didn't consider him a 'slug' when I met him, but I do now."

Marie was very animated as she spoke, arms swinging every which way and a raised voice as if she was yelling at Ben from the inside of a moving vehicle. "Honest to God, Thomas, I don't even know Ben well enough to form such strong feelings, but it's a fact. I hate him for what he is doing to our Hope."

"This story is changing every day. I worry that when Hope gets home she will have to listen to everyone's take on her love life." Marie, with the swinging arms again, interrupted. "In the name of all that is holy, Hope is sixteen years old. *What does she know of love?"*

Wilmot said, "Marie, this really is not our business. We love Hope and we know, at the very least, that she has a serious crush on Ben. We have seen it when they are together. My love, you and I have not met Danielle, so let's leave her out of the conversation. There is so much gossip in the Cape about Ben and Danielle and I think we need to all shut up about it."

Marie simply nodded as she rubbed her husband's shoulder. "I really don't deserve you."

Turning to the back seat, where Thomas and Rescuee were checking each other out, Marie said, "I'm sorry, Ben, Oh God, I meant to say Thomas. Thomas, I am so sorry."

Marie was thankful that Thomas seemed to be amused with her calling him Ben so she sat quietly. Very quietly.

Somewhat muted laughter all around. "Hope and Paradise went to see Lenny before he passed away," Thomas said gently. "They saw him. He passed away. They are coming home. Let's focus on what's important."

24: Age difference

Paradise woke Hope up as the last leg of the journey ended. "Hope, honey, we've been gone for less than a week but it seems longer than that to me. You, too, I bet. It was a lot to take in, and I'm so very proud of how you have dealt with it all. Seeing a friend on their deathbed is never easy."

Paradise was glad she and Hope had had what she had worried would be a heavy conversation about Ben and his 'house guest, Danielle'. She feared Hope would be crushed when she saw Ben with Danielle in the Cape. It was bound to happen.

Hope seemed sure of her feelings for Ben. "He'll be taking courses at the French university up the line while I'm in grade ten! If that sounds a bit creepy to you, can I ask you to look back to when you were in love at sixteen and the boy who said he felt exactly the same way was nineteen? Tell me the truth."

Their 'Ben' discussion ended with Paradise feeling there wasn't anything else she could think of that would help her daughter in the moment. She knew Thomas would have heard about Danielle and likely confronted Ben the same day. Thomas would want to have a discussion with Hope...not until they were behind closed doors in their hotel room, Paradise hoped.

Paradise loved Hope's final thought on the subject, that she shared as she was beginning to cover up with her warm blanket. "When we are old and grey, or as old as you and dad, I will still be three years younger than Ben, but will the three years make a big difference then? I'm going to keep that thought to myself because I don't want to have Ben thinking he just has to wait me out and we will be together. I do want to know how old Danielle is, though. Is that kind of being gossipy, mom? To want to know her age, I mean. I'm more confused than sad about this whole thing. The Ben who held me in his arms at your wedding celebration did not have a fiancée or a girlfriend. I know that in my heart…*my sixteen year old heart*…there, I said it before you did, mother."

"I'm half asleep, Hope. Can we please have this discussion when we wake up?"

"Okay, we can park the topic for now, but when we wake up, will you tell me how you felt about dad when you loved him so much, got pregnant, and he rode off to The Royal Canadian Mounted Police Academy in Regina, leaving you alone to become a nun? A *pregnant Nun*! My God, mother, going off to a convent was a bit extreme, wasn't it? I'm guessing you both knew there was a three-year difference between you, and I'm also guessing that you didn't care about that. Now I'm done. Goodnight, mom."

Paradise wasn't asleep, but she wasn't ready to discuss the age difference between herself and Thomas as compared to Hope and Ben. She kept her eyes and mouth closed and would forever let Hope think her mother hadn't heard that last part of their airplane discussion.

~

More than a dozen hours had passed when they deplaned in Halifax and saw Thomas waving as they stepped onto the escalator that would bring them to the main level for arrivals at the Halifax International Airport, and to Thomas. Paradise had been certain she would have time to explain their Halifax change in plans to Hope. Both of her parents had been summoned to an urgent meeting with Doctor Scott.

It was a long flight, but both Paradise and Hope slept lots and talked lots, and they ran out of time for all they wanted of both. Business is business and Paradise and Thomas had not been paid as much as they would have liked since moving permanently from the US back to Canada. They didn't need millions, but having thousands in the bank would make them sleep a bit easier.

25: Sydney's secret

"Come here, both of you." Thomas hugged his wife and daughter like he had never hugged them before.

"I am so sorry for your loss. My God, that was so fast. You didn't have much time with Lenny I assume, but at least you got to hug him and let him know he was loved. You can tell me all about your trip, the good and the bad of it, at our hotel. It's very close to the airport, so let's go. This way to our car."

Hope was even more confused than before. "Our hotel? Mom, what have you *not* told me?"

Looking at Hope and Thomas, Paradise explained everything. "Thomas and I spoke about this on the phone, however all plans were indefinite so I decided this information could wait. Was I wrong?"

"*Ya think*?" Hope rolled her eyes at both of her parents.

"Hope, that was rude," Thomas said. "Do not do that again, young lady. We have taken today off and we plan to stay right here." As they drove into the hotel parking lot, he said, "Honey, we don't know why, we literally have no details at all, but Doctor Scott has asked that your mother and I meet her at her home as soon as possible. It feels more like a summons than a request to me. Sydney knew we had an emergency of our own."

"I don't think I have the energy to call her," Paradise said. "Lenny's death has taken more than a bit out of me and I worry that if I call, Sydney will sense my weakness and wonder if we are up to the job she is asking of us."

"I'll make the call," Thomas said, "as soon as we are safely in our room and comfortable. There is something going on with Doctor Scott and I'm quite concerned about her health." He thought it would serve no one to guess at what her agenda might hold.

"Oh, one more thing," he added. "I brought your fuzzy, warm housecoats that you love so much. You might like to strip and slip into something very comfortable."

"Dad, no talk about stripping and slipping into something more comfortable when you are about to walk into a hotel room with your bride *and* your daughter." Hope was laughing as she spoke.

As the trio entered their hotel lobby the concierge rushed over with a message from Doctor Scott.

"What's going on Buddy?" Thomas reached out and took the envelope offered to him.

"I believe her memo says it all, but Doctor Scott called and had your things moved to adjoining rooms, so you could all have a bit of space."

"This was so not necessary," Paradise whispered as they made their way to their rooms...two different keys, too.

"Maybe not," said Thomas. "But it's a much appreciated upgrade the day before we hear her urgent news, so let's enjoy it, ladies."

"Roger that."

They all laughed as they responded in unison and then, because it was so funny, they said it again. "Roger that."

"Could I have *my* room key, please?" Hope said. "I have never had my own separate room before so I want the full pleasure of unlocking my own bedroom door. I assume we have a door connecting us inside."

Bit of a drag, thought Hope.

26: Pls prepare for tomorrow

Thomas tried his best to put on a happy face as he walked into the adjoining hotel room, where Paradise and Hope sat cross-legged on the bed, playing cards. He chose his words carefully, but not fast enough to camouflage the shock on his face as he spoke.

"Hope, I need to borrow your mom for a few minutes to bring her up to date about Doctor Scott."

He didn't fool anyone. Paradise jumped off the bed as Hope grabbed a pillow, put it behind her head and leaned back on the headboard. "Dad, you're treating me like a kid again. What's wrong? Is it Sydney? She's my friend too, you know."

"As soon as I talk with your mother we will be back to fill you in. I realize Doctor Scott is a friend to our family, but she was all business when I called her just now. Remember, this is a paid contract your mother and I have with her. It doesn't include sharing with our daughter, regardless of how grown up you are at sixteen." Thomas paused and stepped aside as he suggested Paradise leave the room first.

He didn't like to leave the conversation with his daughter that way. "Hope, you will be pleased to know that Doctor Scott, with all that she has on her plate at the moment, is sending a car for you tomorrow morning. She will confirm the time later this evening. You will have your day in the morgue…you will live another day." Thomas recalled a discussion Doctor Scott had had with Hope when she assured Hope that after visiting her morgue she would live another day. It had become a private joke between student and Doctor.

Hope smiled and nodded. "Go, dad. Talk with mom."

Paradise gestured for Thomas to close the door between their rooms. Maybe not completely shut but enough so Hope would not overhear their conversation. "Why aren't we going to meet with Sydney today? It's not even evening, so we would have lots of time, Thomas."

"Let me tell you what I just learned. I haven't been keeping it from you. It was not easy to keep the little bit I did know from you while you were visiting Lenny, but I figured you had enough on your plate without me adding something else."

Paradise had taken two bottles of beer out of the mini-bar in their room, offered one to Thomas, and sat back on the bed as she opened the second beer and took a swig. "Hit me with it all, starting at the beginning, my love. Sydney must have contacted you shortly after we left."

"Yes, she did. At the time it seemed strange that Sydney reacted the way she did, but now I understand a bit more."

"So share it, already!"

"I spoke with her assistant while you were on your way to Lenny. I tried to get Sydney on the line, but she was not in the building. I hate to admit this, Paradise, but I wasn't overly concerned at the time." Thomas needed another beer.

"Sydney's assistant didn't seem to know why she was not in the office, and, alarmingly, she claimed to not know *where* she was. She offered that not having information about Doctor Scott's location was a first in all the years they had worked together. She always, *always,* knew where Sydney was. It was a commitment to ensure safety for both of them."

Thomas leaned against a wall to stretch his back. "What I'm about to share is disturbing, haunting and criminal. You and I have to take all of this in while considering Hope, when we join her shortly. How much do we tell her now and how much could we keep for our drive back to the Cape tomorrow afternoon?"

Sitting down again, but in a straight-backed chair this time, Thomas continued, "Sydney is desperate to speak with us about three things, all connected. The accused, the young girl that he raped and the trial that won't happen because—"

Paradise jumped in, and regretted it immediately. "What? Thomas, what are you saying?"

"I am trying to explain, my love, so please let me share this without interruption. It's hard to even speak of the horror Sydney has experienced."

"I apologize. Won't happen again."

"Strike two." Thomas stalled because he didn't know how to break it to her gently. There was no easy way.

"The accused was not incarcerated for long pending his trial. I don't know much about the 'outstanding in his community' stuff, because Sydney asked if she could jump over that for now. She could hardly speak the words about how loved the accused was by everyone who knew him. Paradise, that slug found her, and Sydney holds you and me responsible for what happened next. He got right to her door and into her home. That was the urgency she was calling me about. Initially I only told her you had to travel back to Hawaii because a terminal cancer patient wanted to see you before he died. Because she has called almost every single day I have now told her everything about Lenny and Bonde and his death. Sydney and I made these plans that I am about to share,"

Thomas opened his arms wide. "We made these decisions during the call I just made."

"Paradise," Thomas said, "he found out where she lives. He followed her home one evening. She didn't see him right behind her as she unlocked the door. Once she had a single foot in the foyer he pushed her hard enough to knock her down."

"Thomas, you're upset," Paradise said with real concern in her voice. "Do you want to stop for a bit? We could go next door and check on Hope. What would work for you?"

Thomas reached out to give his wife, *his bride,* although their wedding seemed like years ago, a hug before he continued. "Who we will see at Sydney's home in the morning is a woman whose face is unrecognizable due to cuts, swelling, and bruises."

27: Meanwhile, back at the Cape

Lee decided too many people in his world were missing. "Where is my dad? Where is my mom? I know one is in heaven, but I got another one and she isn't here. Where is my sister? Do you think she is missing me as much as I'm missing her?"

All of these questions came while Denis and Waine were still in bed.

The 'deal' Lee had with his two uncles was a simple one. When he was in his bed or in the living room, Lee could speak with either of his Uncles or to both of them at the same time. He did not need to go into their bedroom, or even raise his voice, because the cottage was small enough that you could hear everything through the entire place, regardless of where you were sitting...or the bed you were lying on.

"They will all be home tomorrow night, Lee," Denis said. "If they aren't home by your bedtime, we thought we could take you home so you could sleep in your own bed and we will stay until they arrive. We might even let you stay up past your bedtime. How does that sound?"

"Okay. Can we have lots and lots of boxing today?"

"Yes, we can, and tomorrow we are going to do a few things for your parents, and Hope, before they arrive home. So today it's all about you. Tomorrow it's all about your mom, dad and sister, okay, buddy?"

"Roger that, Uncle Denis. Roger that, Uncle Waine."

There was a short silence. Then: "Hey, can I just ask what we are doing for my parents and Hope? Are we buying them presents or something?'

Waine said, "I believe we are picking their mail up at the post office. Then we will continue on to the store to get a few groceries for their kitchen...just enough to get them through a couple of days in case they need a down day when they get home."

"What's a *pound* day?"

"I said a *down* day."

"What does that mean? I still don't know what they are doing with some sort of a day when they get home."

"That's when you have been working and working and you just need a day on your own, or with the people you love so much," Denis said. "Mainly, you just want to relax and be quiet."

"I have to be quiet on their first day home? That does not seem fair."

Lee was feeling sorry for himself but Uncle Denis and Uncle Waine didn't think he would stay that way for long.

Twenty minutes later all three were in the car, buckled up, and off to find a breakfast spot. Bacon and eggs and toast...lots of toast. The location didn't matter as long as the food was great.

Lee had no idea what was coming after breakfast. He would get to see his new official boxing ring. Lee had seen something being constructed in the centre of the cottage area, but he hadn't asked any questions.

The uncles felt good building this for him. Hope's friend, Ben, donated wood from stuff he had torn out of his home at #8 Cape St Mary Road. They even found something they turned into a tarp large enough to cover the ring when it was not in use. Some fellas up the line at the boat-building site offered to give up an old tarp they were using to cover a huge boat that would leave the yard shortly.

Ben took the proper measurements and the tarp was cut accordingly. He asked the brothers to not mention his involvement if possible. The uncles agreed they would keep it to themselves; but if Hope asked about the boxing ring and who built it, they would have to give Ben a bit of the credit. It seemed right to give credit where credit was due.

28: Sydney

"Paradise, is that a doctor standing in the open doorway at Sydney's home? It's definitely not Sydney." Thomas double-checked the house number just to be certain.

"Something else has happened, Thomas. I just know it. I wonder if Sydney is ill on top of that violent sexual assault."

They turned into her driveway and seconds later they were both on the steps unaware as to how to proceed.

The woman at the door said, "Good morning. I'm Thor, a medical doctor on Doctor Scott's team. I will take you to her in a moment, but she asked me to bring you up to date. Thomas, I am aware that Doctor Scott shared much of her nightmare over the phone last evening. She asked that I review the facts with you since she says she simply cannot go back there in her mind again, at least not this morning. Doctor Scott doesn't have good and bad days. Since the day of her assault she has had bad days only. She tells me that every second of her therapy is painful and exhausting and she hates it. I have been here since the incident took place and will work from here as long as Doctor Scott needs me...certainly for as long as she is unable to attend her offices or the morgue."

"How do we know you're who you say you are?" Paradise said. "She asked us to get here as quickly as possible. Where is she?"

The doctor had an ID card on a lanyard around her neck. She passed it to Paradise, who inspected it closely, then handed it back.

"We will sit in the kitchen, where I have a coffee ready for each of you," the doctor said. "When I finish filling you in I will take you to Doctor Scott. She is expecting you and is anxious to bring you up to date."

Thomas didn't want to sit, but clearly Thor was not happy about that so he took his seat beside Paradise. Thor gave a silent nod of appreciation. "Both Doctor Scott and I are sorry for your loss. We understand you had a dear friend in Honolulu pass away only days ago. We also know—"

Paradise interrupted her. "In the name of God, what is going on with Sydney? I don't understand why you are stalling. Has something else happened since Sydney spoke with Thomas?"

Doctor Thor was on her feet. "I'll be right back. Please do not follow me." She wanted to make sure Doctor Scott realized Thomas and Paradise had arrived. She had become very protective of her boss and her heart ached every time she watched her walk or try to use her arm.

Doctor Scott sat in a big chair delivered personally by her physical therapist, who picked Sydney up every afternoon and took her to a private clinic where she could go without drawing attention to her injuries. She was particularly worried about her eye. No amount of therapy could fix that. It would need a number of surgeries, according to one of her specialists.

Sydney had heard Paradise and Thomas enter her home and she was ready to face them. She gave a nod, and Doctor Thor had her orders. She returned to the kitchen and motioned for Paradise and Thomas to join Sydney in the living room.

Picking up their briefcases and coats they entered the living room together.

Paradise dropped her coffee cup...she had not yet taken one sip.

After a moment of total silence, Sydney said, "Really? I look that bad? And I thought I did a pretty good job with make-up this morning. By the looks on both of your faces it seems I didn't cover much of the damage. Thor, would you mind terribly if I asked you to clean up the spill? And please put another cup of coffee in Paradise's hands."

Turning to her PIs, Sydney said, "Thor is the only person in the house with me this morning, at my request." "My pleasure," Doctor Thor said. "I will be back with my mop and broom *and* a fresh cup of coffee for you, Miss Paradise."

Turning back to her boss, she added, "As directed by you, when I leave you there will be the three of you in the house. Total privacy. However, a couple of us are only seconds away, so if you need anything—"

"Paradise needs her coffee and I need you gone, Thor, so enough with the chatter." Doctor Scott was easily agitated this morning.

Paradise and Thomas were still standing. Thomas took a seat, a sign that Paradise would speak first.

Unable to hide her tears, Paradise said, "My God, Sydney, how did this happen?"

Thomas hadn't yet found his words, so he was happy to remain quiet. He had never seen *anyone* so badly beaten.

"Understand that we have work to do," Sydney said. "However, I'm assuming Doctor Thor neglected to suggest you let me do the talking until I say what I have to say. Paradise, sit down. The very first thing I have to say to the two of you is that you have greatly disappointed me. With you both under personal contract with me in a case revolving around an upcoming trial, I wonder if you will have to shoulder some of this pain and predicament I find myself in? I'm not throwing stones. Just trying to understand. At the very least, how did you miss the part where he was let out of prison pending trial?"

Sydney wanted to continue, but she needed to activate her pain management for the day...all discreetly hidden under her warm bulky jacket. She pressed a button and could almost feel the medication as it went from the needle in her arm directly into her body. This device allowed Sydney, at the very least, to control her medication. Lord knows, she wasn't good for anything at the moment and depression rested on her shoulders, ready to strike.

"This could take awhile, but please do not interrupt me. When I'm truly finished I will end with, 'over to you'. Until you hear those three words, the floor belongs to me. I have yet to share any of this with anyone other than the medical experts who worked on me... and they saw it first-hand, which was much more difficult to view than this morning, believe me. From the time I dialed 911 it would appear I lost consciousness, and when I awoke I was coming out of surgery."

Sydney took a break to sip her coffee and break off a very small piece of her muffin. Looking up at her two confidants, she said, "I'm going to get my thoughts on the record, so I will press the start button on my very old personal tape recorder as I begin. I won't be taping you...this is all about me. I will later try to remember everything I said and then I'll listen to the tape."

With that said, Sydney pressed 'play.'

"Doctor Sydney Scott here, and I am with PIs Paradise and Thomas Adams. I am recording my voice only and for mental health reasons. Eight days ago, someone followed me home from work. It was late in the evening. I had let all of my staff take that night and the next day off because it seems they never catch a break from all that I ask of them. It was a small way to thank them, and I was happy knowing I would have the entire house to myself. I've got this out of order somewhat, but having been in the hospital until my eyes, in particular, were attended to I struggle to remember, and you can only imagine how that upsets me. My wrist was broken in two places thus the cast, and they tell me I will have to wear this reminder of what I have been through for months to come."

Sydney, and Paradise too, wiped tears from their eyes. Thomas knew if he couldn't hold it together this would all have to be done again.

Sydney continued, "As I put the key in my door and opened it, someone directly behind me pushed me with such force that I hurtled forward. I had no idea someone had crept right up behind me, so I did not have my guard up at all. I believe my face hit the floor first, followed by the rest of my body seemingly not attached to my head. Strangest feeling. Never in a million years would I have thought that I would open my eyes and face the man who invaded my life for so many years when I was a teenager. A *very* young teenager. I can see you know whom I'm speaking of. It was him. *Don't say his name please.* I can't stand to even hear it.

"As I scrambled to regain my footing he closed and locked my door. He did it with such drama I wondered for a second if someone on my own team was involved in his attempt to kill me. He knew we were alone in my home. He stood with his hand on the lock but didn't turn it until he was confident I could see him through my already swollen eyes. Only then did I hear the lock fall into place.

"How in God's name did he know I lived here, or that I would be alone in this big house on a particular day and nighttime? I admit, that was a very lonely feeling. How would he have known that if not by someone telling him?"

Sydney paused to sip a bit of water. Even opening her mouth to allow a straw inside seemed to be a bridge too far.

"He wore a face mask and he didn't speak until he finished breaking my wrist. I recognized this double break as something I had seen on other young women murdered through the years. Other coroners on my staff had understood, from the second rape he committed, that he did this both to cause pain and to give him the upper hand in all that he had planned.

"He hadn't spoken, and when I called him by name it surprised him. He removed his mask and I near puked. Confirmation, as if I needed any confirmation that this monster was him. He took his gun out of his vest pocket, and rubbed it on my face. He then put the gun into his pants pocket."

Sydney took a bit of a break while she tried to enjoy a sip of her coffee. "He knew he could overpower me. I soon realized if I had not called him by name, he might have allowed me to live...once he was through with me. It was a very difficult time for me, as you can imagine."

"Oh. My. God. Sydney, I cannot begin to imagine it all..." Paradise thought Sydney might almost welcome the interruption. She was wrong.

"Paradise, I'm beginning to lose my patience with you. Let me continue, and when I finish you will have lots of time to fill me in... including why you did not inform me he was released pending trial. That is specifically what I hired you to investigate, and I would have had one hell of a lot more security in and around my home if you had been doing what I was paying you to do."

Thomas couldn't take his eyes off of Sydney. From what Sydney had shared he guessed the charges would be break and enter, rape, and a beating to the head in an attempt to cause death. Looking at Sydney, sitting stiffly in front of them, he wondered how close she came to death's door and, more specifically, how in God's name she got her hands on the gun.

"I know you both have questions, but I'm almost finished, at least for today. I wasn't conscious for much of the beating but from what my doctors tell me, I was unresponsive but managed to will myself to see out of one eye as this murderer taunted me with talk of his gun. I will never be strong enough to forget what he said and how he said it."

> *"Oh come now, chief coroner, you must be made of stronger stuff than what you have shown here today. I know you can feel my gun every time I rub against you and certainly when I stroke you from the inside. I try to ensure you feel me and my gun every time I rape you. What happened to your pretty face, chief coroner? Did I do that with my kicks to your head, and your face in particular? Oh my, I have definitely re-arranged your face...you were such a pretty little girl back then. What happened to your good looks? Remember our first time together Syd-My-Sexy-Syd and I told you that would be my name for you whenever we were together? Let's play, Doctor Scott. I am going to give you the trip of your life. So here's to raping my Syd one more time."*

"Paradise and Thomas, I knew there would only be one second when I might be able to get to his gun. I knew I would have only one chance, so I played along as much as my broken and battered body would allow. I tried to watch his face but by this time I could barely see. When I thought he might be 'enjoying his climax' rather than watching me, I reached for his gun. I got to it a second before he could grab my hand."

Sydney shifted in her chair, obviously in pain.

"Bang! Bang! Bang! and Bang. The fifth chamber was empty."

~

He had been right. Only one was still breathing. Barely.

Sydney was able to pull the phone down off the telephone table near the back door. She had to crawl to it, and that seemed to take forever. She had little strength left and knew she was about to pass out.

Darkness came the second she finished giving her address to the police. Or had she chatted for some time with the nice young lady on the phone? Confusion set in.

Every policeman and woman who responded to the call was in shock at the scene they found.

Soon machines were keeping her alive while surgical specialists worked to set her broken bones and put her eye back where it belonged. Fortunately, there was no brain bleed and there was no swelling of the brain, although this could change at any time. While she slept they put her body together again.

~

"Thomas and Paradise, in case there is any doubt: I shot and I killed the bastard. We both had our hands all over the gun, but the only area where they could not find a definitive print was on the trigger itself. My fingerprint on the trigger was smudged when he tried to take the gun away from me."

29: 0800 sharp

When Paradise and Thomas entered the adjourning bedroom they found Hope fully dressed and filling her backpack one more time. “We’re not staying here tonight, are we? I just assumed we were going home later today. I saw your note about going to the morgue when I got out of the shower.”

With a smile Hope continued, “I’m ready to leave ahead of you two, for a change. Can one of you pat me on the back since my hands are busy?”

Paradise was happy to oblige.

“We’re all set as well, honey,” she said, “so let’s get ourselves downstairs and watch for your driver. 0800 is fast approaching.”

“Hope,” Thomas said, “we will take your backpack with us. We are driving to Doctor Scott’s house and, later in the day your driver will bring you to us.”

The trio stepped off of the elevator, and there stood a well-suited young man holding a sign that read, ‘Miss Hope.’ One more hug for her mom and dad, and Hope was off on her adventure.

She had questions as she and the young man left the hotel and walked toward a car. *It’s very long and very black and just what the Chief Coroner might drive around in*, she thought.

“Where should I sit?”

“You have a choice, miss. You can have the privacy of the back seat or you are welcome to join me up front.”

“How long will the drive be?” Hope realized she might be asking too many questions as her excitement increased.

"I'll have you at your destination before 0900, miss."

"Does everyone associated with Doctor Scott speak as formally and *clipped* as you do, sir?"

"Say again? *Clipped*, you say? I thought I was being all-professional-like. It's not every day that I drive anyone but Doctor Scott. When I drive the Doctor, she works the entire time so there is no talking. *Absolutely no talking*."

"You know my name. And, your name would be...?"

"I'm Chuck. Have you made a decision, Miss Hope? Front or back seat? I can't deliver you to your destination by 0900 if you aren't in my car within the next few minutes."

"Handsome and a smart ass! Just my type. If I had a type, I mean. Pardon me, Chuck, I'm not hitting on you, I don't even know if I'm using the expression correctly. I think I'm just nervous about meeting my first dead person. Front seat, please"

"I would be nervous, too, going downstairs to the morgue. I've never been, and I have no desire to. You'll make an excellent first impression on all the dead folks you meet, I'm sure," said Chuck as he waited for Hope to buckle her seat belt.

Hope knew Chuck was trying to make her less nervous and thought that was sweet. "I'm sixteen, Chuck, how old are you?"

"Miss Hope, I am exactly double your age so in your world I believe you would call me old."

"But, in *your* world you're *not* old, is that what you are saying?"

"That is exactly what I'm saying, young lady." Chuck attempted to change the subject. "If you look off to your right, that monster of a building off in the distance is your destination for the day. It's closer than it looks because, of course, I know all the shortcuts."

"I will be driving you to Doctor Scott's residence when she calls me," he continued. "I suspect it will be several hours from now, but not more than that. I know you and your parents have a bit of a drive to your home later today."

"How do you know where we live? That's not a bad thing, but if your directions for today were merely to drive me to the morgue and then to Doctor Scott's residence, how would our home location come up? My parents are Private Investigators, so I've learned to ask questions. Lots of questions, and I apologize if I have asked too many."

"You can save a question or two for our drive later."

Chuck turned into a driveway and Hope immediately saw several security guards. "I am going to park directly in front of the front door to the offices of our Chief Coroner and like magic..." Chuck clapped his hands and the front door opened.

"Cool. Very cool," said Hope as a woman emerged from the monster building and approached the car on the passenger side. She smiled and opened the car door for Hope.

"Good morning, Hope. Welcome to our little world inside this massive building. It's impressive on the outside, but inside you will find a maze of offices from top to bottom. Lots of office doors are pretty much always closed, but I know the ones we are allowed to open for your tour. I'm Lois, by the way. Let's get you inside."

Hope jumped out of the car, thanked Chuck, and was ready but nervous to see dead people.

Lois had a 'guest pass' ready for Hope and encouraged her to clip it where everyone could see it. "We do give tours to students a couple of times a year, but they are given a very specific tour and as part of a group."

"Lois, I feel bad now. Am I interrupting your day?"

"Honestly, yes you are. However, I'm thrilled to be showing you our little world here, and perhaps teaching you several things as well."

Lois took Hope directly to her office so she could see her area, and then they would go into the Chief Coroner's suite.

Hope was impressed. If this was the office belonging to a secretary, what would the larger offices look like?

Lois motioned for Hope to move to the window seats. Hope plopped down and fell into the most comfortable overstuffed chair ever. Without thinking she said, "Oh. My. God. This is so comfortable. I could die in this chair."

"Oh, please don't do that," Lois said with a chuckle. "I know the extensive paperwork required when a deceased enters via our morgue. I can only imagine the paperwork required if you die in my office so please...just don't."

Hope could hardly contain herself.

"Hope, let's get you down to the morgue first. That's the reverse of how we would handle a tour. But you've mentioned *the dead* a few times so maybe you would be able to enjoy the rest of the tour if we started from the bottom up."

"Sure, but I'm scared. Don't tell my mother, please, because I have wanted to visit a morgue since I was a kid."

"I need you to be less hyped when we enter the morgue, Hope, so I'll give you some useless information to help return your heart rate to normal before we head to the morgue. First of all, and you might know this already, when you hear that someone is a 'medical examiner', or 'ME', he or she has been appointed to the position. The ME must have completed training in pathology to be able to investigate deaths that occur under suspicious circumstances. Postmortem examinations are most often completed by a medical examiner. As it pertains to Doctor Scott, she is both Medical Examiner and chief coroner. Hope, she is, without exception, the smartest person I know. Her memory is incredible. And organized...I'll save that for another time, when the dead are not awaiting us."

"Maybe I'll write a paper about Doctor Scott as a school project next term." Hope was writing everything down as fast as she could.

"I only met her in person once, at my parent's wedding, but we spoke on the phone before that, when she called needing to talk to mom. She would tell you I was rude. A bit, maybe. I apologized, though, and I'm not ever bringing that conversation up with her again."

"Hope, I can say with total honesty that Doctor Scott had never mentioned you until she called from her home late yesterday to say you would be 'delivered' to me at 0900 hours this morning and I was to spend every second with you...so here we are."

Hope stood up. "Lead the way, Lois. I'm ready."

30: Homecoming misplaced

A small crowd slowly gathered at 548 Cape St Mary Road. The evening before Thomas left for the city to meet up with his wife and daughter, Pops had casually mentioned that he might tell a few folks what day and a guess at what time the family would arrive. After all, this was a huge homecoming for young Lee, who had bunked in with Uncles Denis and Waine for *too-many-nights*, as Lee explained to anyone who would listen.

Lee even invited Ben to come to the party, but Ben explained he didn't think this would be wise. Lee didn't understand what that was all about, and his uncle Waine said he didn't understand it, either. Uncle Denis said sometimes when you don't understand something, it means it's none of your business anyway.

"Okay, now I understand. It's none of my business, right?" Lee said.

End of discussion as all three men pushed away from their tiny table and reached for their boxing gloves.

En route to the boxing ring Uncle Denis explained to Lee that it was never a good idea to have a big meal right before you box. They had gotten used to boxing just before suppertime. "We had errands to run today so we could have a few decorations to hang at 548 and a little bit of junk food around, because that's always a good idea when bachelors like us are in charge of what the 'nibbles' food should or shouldn't be. Just back me up if anyone references our choice of Coke and Sloppy Joe's for everyone."

"Roger that," said Uncle Wayne.

'Roger that," offered Lee but it seemed he had more to say, using words as only a five year old could. "I get why we should not have a big supper right before we box, but, ummm..." Lee seemed unsure of what he wanted to say; yet he continued. "But then why did both of you have five hotdogs each...every one of them with a bun, too? I counted everything up when I saw the package in the garbage empty and the label said there were twelve hotdogs inside. *Twelve.* I had two but just one bun. That's how I figured out how many you two ate." Lee wasn't sure if he should continue or shut up.

"*Are you both bawling?* Am I in trouble?" One uncle threw Lee in the air and the other uncle caught him. "Guess not," said Lee laughing, and pretending to box with each of them.

After the three men at #3 Cabin completed their boxing-before-bedtime routine, a fast shower times three was next. Denis and Waine wanted to do a good job as hosts for this shindig, so next they made a list of who would most likely be at the party. They hadn't been sure how to make the RSVP idea work, so they didn't ask anyone to let them know if they were or weren't able to come.

Funny enough, they were pretty confident a lot of the Cape family would come out to support their friends at 548 Cape St Mary Road in this dark time. Most of the locals knew Lenny from when he tracked Paradise down and worked any jobs he could find so he could stay around for a while. Everyone had liked Lenny: he flew below the radar, didn't say much to anyone but Paradise. They walked along Mavillette beach together every morning at sunup.

"We make up three and they make up three so we have six already, right?" Lee was excited to see his parents, and Hope, too. He really missed his sister.

Denis continued with the count. "Wilmot and Marie, Mrs. Foss because she's on her property in her cottage for several more days."

"And mom's old friend, Elise," Lee said. "Mom really likes Elise. They cry all the time but mom told me they cry 'good' tears."

"Okay," Denis said. "And there's no reason why we wouldn't invite the twins, I assume?"

"Well, I'll probably have to baby-sit them during the party," Lee said. "I don't know if I'll get paid, though. Shouldn't a kid get paid if he does a good job babysitting someone's kids because they want to have fun at a party?"

In unison the uncles said, "Ask your mother, young man."

~

As Thomas put their car's signal light on and turned right on to Cape St Mary Road, not a word was said about the first house they passed. Ben's lights were all off and his car was not there.

Paradise turned to the back seat to gauge her daughter's mood in the moment. Hope gave her a two-thumbs up. Their eye contact spoke volumes about the bond they shared.

But both Thomas and Paradise began to worry as they approached car after car after car parked before and past their home. Their entire driveway and yard had just one parking spot available...they were grateful for that.

Paradise turned to Thomas. "Didn't you say Pops asked if he could invite a few...*a few*...of our friends and neighbours to help him greet us at the door?"

As she spoke, Lee was almost flying through the door and out to the car. Thomas motioned for him to go to his mother's side to hug her first. This gave Thomas a second or two to talk with Pops.

"Pops, I love you for this, but Paradise and Hope have just returned from their trip to see Lenny only minutes prior to his death. Paradise and I met with a very traumatized client for four hours this morning, and here we are...bone tired yet appreciative to have you in our lives. Can we move this party to cabin #3? It will spill outside anyway, but I'm assuming Russ is in there." He pointed to Russ and Carol's home. "They have chairs they might be able to let us borrow. I will keep us busy with Lee until I see you come out of our home, and that will be a sign that you spoke to everyone and they agreed to the move. Immediately."

"For once, young man, I'm ahead of you. Eugenie was all over me, and not in a good way, as your house filled up, so we can make the move. The good thing about having Denis and Wayne arrange this party has been that the bags of chips, peanuts, tacos and dips have not been opened yet. I hope one of you can come over for a drink, but I will leave that entirely up to you."

In his haste to speak with everyone, it took Pops a second or two to see his good wife, herding folks out the side door. Yesterday Eugenie had tried to tell him this was not a good idea, and Pops was glad his wife wasn't one of those 'I told ya' people.

Eugenie marched everyone out the side door as if she had done this her entire life, then turned to Pops. "Our wonderful neighbours have carried out whatever they brought in. so I'm hoping they won't see much of a mess. Meet me at the back door, Pops."

"Roger that" said Pops. He had never loved or appreciated his wife more.

With a huge smile on his face, Pops reopened the front door. For a brief moment he was the town crier, a soft-spoken town crier, as he declared:

> Hear ye
> Hear ye
> Hear ye
> Your home awaits, my lady...

Paradise replied with a silent thank-you. She held Lee in one arm, with her other arm around Hope.

Thomas gathered the luggage and, as a family of four, they walked into their empty home.

"Thank you, God," Paradise whispered.

Thomas couldn't let the moment pass. "Thank you to Pops as well for making several dozen friends and neighbours disappear."

Hope offered to take Lee to his bedroom and lie down with him until one or both of them fell asleep.

~

That same day, several hours earlier, Doctor Scott had interrupted her private investigators, saying she needed a brief washroom break. That was not true. She needed time to contact her driver and ask him to deliver Hope immediately. She knew Paradise and Thomas would want to finish this discussion before leaving her. Feeling totally let down by them, Doctor Scott didn't much care what they wanted.

She knew she was letting emotions rule her mind and heart as she returned to the living room. The PIs were seated, as if they knew what was coming. They had already put most of their notes away.

"As I mentioned, I am very disappointed in your commitment to my safety. Therefore, I will no longer require your services. You may send me your final invoice."

Doctor Scott's voice was a high-pitched sound and the PIs were at a loss for words.

"I have spoken with my driver and Hope will be delivered here at any moment. I will terminate this meeting and you can wait in the kitchen...same door you entered. I will leave you to it."

Doctor Scott turned, took the few stairs to her private quarters, entered her bedroom and locked the door behind her. Only then did she allow the tears to fall.

As the PIs moved to the kitchen as directed Thomas reached out for Paradise. He had been in the city for twenty-four hours before she and Hope arrived home and he had spent his entire time searching for details about the upcoming trial. He had found nothing. How and who was in charge of keeping Sydney's nightmare out of the newspapers? And, the deceased…nothing said about him either?

"Sweetheart," he said, "let's make the trip home all about Hope's experience. If we start talking about this case it could upset her. Let's drive home, say hello to Pops and Eugene and anyone else in our home, and then kick them all out."

"Roger that," Paradise said through her tears. "But one question, and be totally honest with me. If I had not gone to Honolulu, would this have happened? How could anyone know of our plans, especially since our plans changed in Kentville when you called us at the Café with news about Lenny's health?"

"Dry those tears, my love. Hope is here." Thomas wiped his tears as well.

31: Enter Doctor Langille

Very early the following morning, Sydney was surprised and not happy to hear repeated knocks on the door to her private quarters. A quick look via her television monitor didn't make her any happier, but at least this guest would not be armed.

"Lois, I did *not* ask you to come to my home. I believe you know that I will be working from home for some time and want no visitors. *None.* What part of that directive is difficult to understand? You also know I would be meeting with private investigators at some point and was not to be disturbed. Since you are here, to give you a brief update, I *have fired* the pair of them! Lois, I'm telling you this because you could be next to go if you keep coming to my home. Unannounced and not called for by me personally isn't that hard a directive to follow, is it?"

Sydney realized she was shaking and shouting at her Executive Assistant. But she couldn't seem to stop herself, and continued with a voice she did not recognize. "Who gave me away? If it was one of the PIs? I swear to God I will get in their faces so fast—"

"It was *not* Paradise or Thomas. This is so not like you, Sydney, and furthermore I have taken the liberty of asking your newly appointed psychologist to join us here. Imagine my surprise to hear that you fired your first-appointed psychologist for being honest, as I understand it. Saying all of this will get me fired for certain. Should I just leave?"

Lois had no plans to leave Sydney's home. As she slowly backed out of the room she collided with a tall and lanky man who was literally right behind her.

Lois stumbled but caught herself before she fell. "I assume you are Doctor Sydney's new therapist? I see that Sydney recognizes you, but if I could see some identification, before I leave you with this woman who has become a sister to me, I would appreciate it. Call me overprotective, but I will never again let a day pass without ensuring that this lady right here is safe."

Lois moved back into the room and with a pointed finger stabbed Sydney in her shoulder. Then she stepped aside to allow Doctor Langille to enter.

Doctor Gary E Langille saw what Lois did not see. *Her eyes showed only fear.*

The doctor's doctor spoke in such a soft voice that Lois wasn't sure Sydney would be able to hear what he was saying. "Look at me. Sydney. *Look into my eyes.* I am not going anywhere until we talk. When Lois poked you in the shoulder it felt like the barrel of a gun to you. I recognized it the instant she touched you. She was being kind, actually, so you have nothing to fear."

Sydney said, "That is confidential information, Lois. And while I applaud your asking for credentials, there is no need. This gentleman is, indeed, my new psychologist, so you are leaving me in good hands."

Sydney attempted to smile but her face wasn't working at the moment. "One more thing, Lois: can I hire you back? Please show up tomorrow."

And with a small wave of her 'good' hand, she dismissed Lois.

Lois turned and made a fast exit, because she knew if this was about whoever beat her boss up and left her for dead, Lois did not want to hear a word about it. She knew nothing, and that was fine with her. Her boss would fill her in when the time was right.

Doctor Langille smiled as he observed Doctor Scott attempting to be, or pretending to be, relaxed. Gary could see she was rather agitated, and thought his presence, a month or two earlier than planned, might be the cause.

Gary did not come to his new client with any information previous to the day of her attack. He needed nothing more, for now. He had received a brief call from Lois telling him Sydney had fired her former therapist because she wouldn't 'leave Sydney alone.'

Understandably, Gary was trying to tread lightly.

32: Ben has hope

If your God in heaven is watching over you this morning, Hope, I hope he or she sits on my shoulder as I attempt to get through this before you kick me out.

Earlier that morning Thomas and Paradise stopped at #8 Cape St Mary Road long enough to tell Ben they were off to Yarmouth for groceries and some odds and ends they most likely would find at a local thrift shop. They would be a couple of hours, maybe more and Hope had asked her dad to tell Ben she was ready to hear what he had to say for himself.

"Ben, Hope and her mom have had a rough week, as you may have heard. They are both pretty fragile. Hope will listen to what you have to say, but then she might ask you to leave; and, by God, if you don't do what she asks of you, I'll be back. Understood?"

Attempting to lighten the discussion, Ben decided he would quote Hope so he simply said, "Sure." Then he walked with Thomas to the door.

Paradise saw the two men shake hands. She would ask Thomas about that at another time.

Lee sat patiently in the back seat, asking why they had stopped already. "Why is Ben coming with us? Does he need groceries, too? Is Ben's eye still bruised after I whooped him in the ring? It was a mistake, mommy, honest to God. Is Ben coming with us or not?"

Turning to look at Lee, Paradise said, "Inside voice, remember, Lee?"

After they had been apart for over a week, Lee had started calling her 'mommy' instead of his normal 'mom', so Paradise had been extra kind and used nothing but her own inside voice with Lee whether they were inside or on Mavillette beach. "Ben is not coming, sweetheart, but he wants to see Hope, so your dad is telling him she is at the house now."

"I hope he doesn't tell Hope that he paid for everything we needed to build our boxing ring. He made us promise we would never ever tell Hope about all the stuff he did for us. He built the ring all by himself, too. My uncles and I pretended we were helping but Ben said we were in the way. He was laughing when he said it, so I laughed, too."

~

As the song says, 'and then she heard the knock on upon the door.' Hope had seen his car pull into their driveway. She was watching for him and was glad he was here.

Her life had been so busy she hadn't had much time to think about Ben and how he had broken her heart in a million pieces. However, once they returned to Clare and their home at 548 Cape St Mary Road, Hope had thought of nothing but Ben. She hadn't been able to get the image of them together out of her mind: Ben, wearing his unbuttoned jeans and her, whoever she was, wearing his unbuttoned shirt.

She would listen…just listen.

With a sweeping arm motion, Hope opened the door and motioned for Ben to come inside. She had a smile on her face, but Ben knew her well enough to know she had pasted that smile on her face just before she opened the door.

"Hope, thank you for agreeing to see me. Regardless of how you view me, or what you think you know about me, I'm begging you to please listen to me so I can tell you everything."

"Sure," came the reply. Ben suspected he would get a lot of single-word responses from Hope this morning.

He immediately saw two plastic placemats on the table, directly across from each other, each with a mug and a paper napkin, so he quickly sat down.

As she picked up her mug, Hope asked, "Coffee?"

Two can play this game, thought Ben, so he decided he would also use one-word responses where he could. It might make Hope smile. He thought she looked frail and he hoped he hadn't been the cause of that. She also appeared nervous around him, and that broke his heart.

"Sure," he said.

Hope sat her mug back down and reached for his while being careful not to touch him. "Black?"

"Thanks," Ben replied.

"Talk," said Hope.

"Sure."

"Now."

With her last reply, Hope had spoken volumes. She seemed a bit sharp, so Ben quickly made sure he had his thoughts in order.

He took one more sip of coffee and began. "First, and most important for both of us, is that when I first met you during your parents' wedding reception, I was and still am single. I promise you that and I can see you are going to interrupt me. Please don't, Hope. I have to get through this, okay?"

"Okay."

Ben tried to sip his coffee while making sure he wasn't smiling.

"When my parents died in the car crash I was completely shattered. If it hadn't been for my university friends, who refused to leave me alone, I'm not sure I would have recovered. When two policemen and a priest knocked at my dorm room, many of my friends were right behind them. They had seen the flashing police lights and gathered to ask if someone was sick, could they help in some way. They later shared that, the minute the priest told me my parents had died, I fainted. Hit the floor before anyone could catch me. That's when they set up the a schedule so I wouldn't be alone until after the funeral. I can tell you more about that another time. I know that what, or who, you need to talk about right now is Danielle."

"Bingo," said Hope.

"Danielle and I dated through our last year of high school. Following that, we both took a gap year and travelled with our parents...*not* with each other. Our parents have always wanted us to get together, and they would tell us that we could be as happy as they were. We didn't buy into their theory. I don't remember the details of how we broke up, but I'm getting ahead of myself."

Ben needed more coffee.

"Everyone in my class had a girlfriend or boyfriend, and I wanted one, too. Danielle had asked me out a number of times, but I always seemed to be busy. We talked about this when she surprised me with her visit here. We were close and, yes we were intimate, but we didn't continue any type of relationship after our final year of high school. I suspect her parents called her to deliver the news about my parents, and they probably suggested she should come home for the funeral. Her mother came to the house often once I got home from university. That's how I learned Danielle was studying in Switzerland but she would be coming home for the funeral. She attended with her parents, who had been best friends with my parents. The three of them came back to our house and they were the last to leave. They wanted to make sure my university friends got back on that huge bus that everyone on my street wanted to complain about."

Standing up, Ben asked if he could have a very brief washroom break. He promised he would then begin his story with the day Danielle surprised him in Cape St Mary.

33: Hope has heard enough

"I know when you walked into my place and saw Danielle there you felt you had 'caught us together,' not knowing any of the circumstances."

"Dare I hope you have saved the best for the last...best news, I mean?" Hope offered a real smile for the first time through a very long, miserable and informative one-way discussion. She needed more.

"Have you just gone from one word answers to about fifteen words in a single sentence?"

Ben wanted to reach out and wipe away the tears on her cheek, but Hope moved away from his reach.

For no reason other than the fact that their kitchen chairs were not the most comfortable, Ben asked, "Is there any way we could move this discussion into the living room Hope? Perhaps even to the love seat facing the ocean."

"NO."

Ben realized he had made Hope angry simply by asking what seemed to him a pretty reasonable question. "Okay. Danielle's mother and my mother had apparently talked about how they were certain we would find our way to each other. And that when one of our mothers passes away before the other, the surviving mother was to take possession of the deceased's engagement ring. This was only to be shared when we, Danielle and me, 'found each other.' Danielle had learned this when she came home for mom and dad's funeral. Her mother had taken mom's engagement ring from her jewellery box. I had put it away there until I had time to go through everything, piece by piece, and then decide what I wanted do with it. I hadn't even looked inside, to be honest."

Hope passed the box of tissues, because now Ben was crying, too. "I am not proud of this, Hope, but when Danielle shared this story and then pushed her ring finger in my face to show me she was already wearing my mom's ring, I lost it. I called her a liar. I said she must have stolen it and we got into a huge shouting match. I'll spare you the details. I didn't have the heart to kick her out that late at night, so I gave her my bedroom, and I slept on the living room floor. When you came in I was having trouble getting into my jeans because I ached all over from sleeping on the floor. *Alone on the floor.*

"I can't speak for Danielle, but she was getting cleaned up in the bathroom when you arrived. When she came out in one of my shirts and nothing else I was as surprised as you were. When she tried to provoke you by showing you my mother's engagement ring on her left hand I could hardly breathe. She took the ring off of her finger the previous evening and gave it to me. I made the mistake of leaving it in the bathroom...inside my shaving kit, where I didn't think she would see it. Almost finished, I promise."

Ben got himself a glass of water. Hope was not taking her eyes off him until she heard everything.

"Hope, after you and your mother left, I very calmly asked Danielle for her parents' phone number so that I could update my files. I did write it down, but I also dialed their number when Danielle was getting dressed, which she should have done before coming out of the bathroom when she heard your voice." Ben downed his glass of water.

"I had a couple of minutes with her mom before Danielle was dressed and looking for me. I had taken the phone, thanks to the ridiculous long cord that was here when I moved in, to the stoop near the front door. Danielle's mom was pleasantly surprised to hear from me. I said I wanted to ask her a few questions but first I wanted to make sure Danielle was with me so she would hear our conversation without me telling her after the fact. To say her mom was shocked to learn Danielle was here would be an understatement. She was almost hysterical. I could hear her husband speak to her in that soft voice he always uses with his wife. I asked Danielle to join me when she was dressed."

"Are you talking with your other girlfriend behind my back?"

"No, Danielle. I'm speaking with your mother."

Total silence.

"You are *not* speaking with my mother, but I'll play along, Hey, ma. Have you noticed that the engagement ring is missing...again?"

Danielle's father grabbed the phone. "Don't you speak to your mother in that tone ever again, do you hear me?"

"I do, daddy, but Ben called you without telling me and I thought he was joking like he always does with me. You both know how tight we are, right?"

Ben took the phone and went back inside, slamming and locking the door behind him."Sir, I am not, nor have I ever been, engaged to your daughter. She tells me my mother wanted her to have her engagement ring, but that makes no sense to me. When she knocked on my door, I was shocked. Danielle continues to shock me with her stories about your and my parents, and how you think she is in Switzerland and will never find out she came to Canada to 'reunite' with me. Sir, she has rented a very high-end luxury car and pays no attention to the roads here. She seems to feel she is above everything and everyone and that she's the safest driver around here. It's not true, of course, and I am worried for her safety when she packs up and is on her way."

Ben could hear Danielle's mother encouraging her father to tell him something. He sat and listened to them for a minute or two. He was surprised that Danielle had not tried the front door, so he looked out the window and saw her in her rental car.

It seemed her mother had taken ownership of the phone. "Ben, is Danielle right there beside you?"

"Danielle is spread out on the back seat of her rental. She appears to be sleeping, which is nuts because she just got up a couple of hours ago. Does she have bouts of passing out? I hope you won't 'shoot the messenger', but Danielle acts like she's on something."

"Ben, after high school you took the high road and she took another road. In the last few years we have had our beautiful daughter in every clinic around the world, where they have all tried to help Danielle help herself. She is supposed to be in Switzerland in a lock-down facility where she is getting the best treatments possible for narcotics addiction."

Ben tried to wrap it up because he knew Paradise and Thomas would most likely be home soon. He shared with Hope how Danielle's parents asked him to pack her belongings, because the police would be there soon. They would arrange everything.

"I have no idea how it happened, but before I could go outside to check on Danielle, they were in my yard. I heard men speaking to her. She was not responding. Or I couldn't hear her. I found drugs in her suitcase so I put them in the outside pouch of her carry-on. Hope, this, all of this, broke my heart for her mother and father."

Ben pulled a card from his pocket and dropped it on the table. "One of the men is not a policeman. I know him; his name is Elroy. That's his card from Worldwide Narcotics Addiction Reform. I did find literature with a heading of WNAR in Danielle's suitcase. We both box at the newest, and perhaps only, boxing ring in Cape St Mary. We are pretty evenly matched and enjoy sparring with each other when Elroy's schedule allows him down time. His said they would take Danielle to a facility equipped to help her for the short term. When she is stable, her father will come to take her home."

"That's it. I've heard enough." Hope offered a smile and held out her hand. "Let's you and I go for a walk on Mavillette Beach before the gang arrives home, which would mean Lee would have to come with us. In fact, let's run to the beach. Then we can walk."

Ben thought he would never be happier than he was in that moment holding Hope's hand.

"You're quite the story-teller, Ben. Thank you for sharing everything with me. That is *everything,* correct?"

Ben turned to hug Hope, who met him with another 'NO', as loud as the one he was served at the kitchen table earlier.

"I'm not sure I want a boyfriend right now, but I don't want you to be mad at me either. My mind has been all over the place. Did you know Lenny died?"

"I did," replied Ben. "Your dad told me. I'm sorry, I know you were fond of Lenny and didn't mind your mom walking on the beach with him almost every day."

"That's true. Lenny always thought that one day she would wake up and realize it wasn't Thomas she wanted but him...Lenny."

"I may not like it, but I do get the comparison to us. At least, I think I do. I'll leave it alone for now, if that's okay with you. Let's enjoy this fabulous day with each other, even if it ends before we want it to. By that I mean Lee might come running at us at any minute."

"Actually, my parents would never let Lee come down to the beach to find me. He would walk directly out and dive into this ocean, I swear. This kid has no fear of anything, including water. Believe me, I have intentionally walked behind Lee en route to the beach and when he takes a quick look over his shoulder and thinks he's alone he runs straight into the water at high tide."

"Do you have any fears, Hope?" Ben was sure he knew what she would say and that's what he wanted to talk about. But it had to be Hope who brought it up.

34: Doctors Scott and Langille

"Do you know what I hate about therapy?"

Doctor Langille was happy to play along because this sounded like a joke was coming his way. "I have no idea, Doctor Scott, but I suspect you are going to tell me. And, by the way, I'd feel better if we go with 'Sydney' and 'Gary' at this stage, if that works for you."

"First names are fine with me, especially in my own home. Please let me get this out before you hit me with your best shot."

Gary was pleased with the lightness of her voice. "Sydney, the floor is yours. Please tell me anything...almost anything, since it's our first day together."

"What I hate about therapy is *the pity that comes with it*. 'Oh, poor Sydney is in Gary's office again.' You know this is true, Gary. Until we give mental health a chance through therapy, the stigma will not go away."

"I don't disagree with you, Sydney. Now, let's get some hard work done. Talk to me."

"I have hurt so many people that I deeply care for. I appreciate I was not myself after enduring rape and beatings that almost broke me. However, Doctor, I have to face facts. I can't hide at home forever. I even miss working with my 'clients' who rent a slab while waiting for their autopsy."

"Can you talk to me about your physical injuries, Sydney? My job as your therapist extends well beyond mental issues. You know that." Gary introduced this line of discussion as gently as possible.

He wanted Sydney to keep talking, but she needed to move the discussion to the 'visible' that staff would see the second she returned the work.

"I'm not talking about today, Gary. I'm not stupid. You must know this is not my first rodeo—"

"It *is* your first rodeo, Sydney, throwing around words like rape, beatings, unconsciousness, murderer, murdered…and using all of the above in the *first person.*" "Please let me continue *and* conclude before you open that mouth of yours. Haven't you been taught to not interrupt others, or at the very least to not interrupt me?" Sydney offered the last comment with the hint of laughter.

With an imaginary 'zipping of his mouth,' Gary sat back, and got comfortable.

"Gary, God help you if you interrupt me again. To speak with you regarding my physical condition is painful. I feel weak and violated and I fear that you, and others as they see me, will pity me. I don't think I could stand that."

Gary couldn't help himself. "What a pity, doctor."

"I set myself up for that, and surprisingly I do appreciate humour during this discussion. You and I have worked with each other through too many cases to count during the last twenty-five years. Humour affords me a second or two to gather my thoughts. I have lots to share, if it's really my visible injuries we are talking about here today."

With a nod from Gary, Sydney continued. "The most obvious is my somewhat dangling eye. I have already had two surgeries on it since this happened, and if things move in the right direction there will be a third and possibly final surgery within the month. I will return to work with a few pairs of sunglasses. I realize the look of my face is startling in so many ways, but you wouldn't believe how many doctors are working to put me back together again. 'Plastics' are up next, according to my GP, who is quarterbacking all of the doctors involved in my case. It takes an army, Gary." This time it was Sydney offering the humour.

"May I speak now?"

"Yes you may." Sydney sat up poker-straight, with her good hand gently on top of her broken wrist, and waited for Gary to deliver his best shot.

"Sydney, I read in your file that your arm was broken in two *signature* locations, wrist and upper arm. I understand that 'signature' refers to the way this bastard took control over each of his victims so you couldn't fight back."

Sydney realized Gary was weaving the discussion about her physical injuries together with her mental state and, for now, she was willing to follow his lead. "Yes, we couldn't have a pillar of the community returning home to his wife and children through the years with scratches all over his face. The more the team putting me back together spoke of this exact double break of an arm and wrist of multiple victims I remembered more than a few very young women, girls really, who presented in my morgue with the same breaks that I have. Only God knows the final count."

"Thank you for sharing this level of detail. This will help us as we move forward. Can you tell me about the gun? I read about the assailant playing his dirty little game of rubbing his body, the pocket holding his gun in particular, against your groin area with his gun just out of reach. Can you think back and tell me what you were thinking in that moment?"

"At first, I didn't understand what he was saying. 'Only one of us will manage to get to the gun. Only one person will live.' His words are now seared into my brain. With the ongoing beating I was taking, I knew I was not thinking rationally or quickly. Second by second I willed myself to gain strength just for a few more minutes. I would have to move my groin region in the right direction at the right time and fast enough to get to the gun first and slow enough to keep him from catching me until it was too late. He violated me again and again and again.".

She stood shakily. "Sorry, Gary, I need a drink so I am going to pretend it's five o'clock and pour myself a brandy. What about you, doctor? Can you have a drink while on the clock?"

Gary smiled at this brave, courageous and super-intelligent woman. "We are almost finished for today, so, if you wouldn't mind pouring me a glass of whatever you're having, I won't touch it until I ask my last question."

"That sounds like you are about to ask me a pretty flat last question, doctor.' Sydney put his brandy on the small table beside his chair. "I'll grant you one more question, so go ahead. Cheers."

"Let's talk about clarity and your mental state as you reached for the gun in his pocket and instantly felt his hand on top of yours." Gary paused, hoping this *wasn't* his last question of the day.

"I certainly wasn't the one with the advantage in the fight. The gun was on my right side, with my broken and tattered arm and hand. Of course, this had been well thought out so he could taunt me until he killed me. I asked questions to try to keep him talking. I had calculated that my best opportunity to turn things around would be if, for a second, the gun would be at my wrist level. I knew I would need the supernatural strength we hear about that comes to individuals as they near death's door. I timed my move for the nano-second when he climaxed. God was with me. I leaned in to him, got to the gun first, and it was my finger on the trigger. I remember that he had his hand over mine in less than a second and he was attempting to move my hand away. The first shot might have been accidental because, and this came as a welcomed surprise to me, I had more strength than he did even with my broken arm. I wasn't sure he was dead, so I moved the gun towards his heart and fired again. The third bullet did the most visual damage. I shot him in the face. I can tell you that because you can't repeat anything that would break client-doctor privilege. Now, in the name of God, can we stop for the day?"

Gary looked back through his notes, reached for his drink and took a sip before he spoke. "We can certainly leave this for next time, but you mentioned you tried to ask questions that might give you a bit more time to get your body closer to the gun. Can you think back and share one or two of the questions you asked?"

"Your query is bigger than a breadbox, doctor, and that might not make sense until I answer your question. I first met the deceased when I had just turned 15. I can't go any further today, and you *will* understand. I promise I will try to tell you everything.

"You've done splendidly today, Sydney, and I am very impressed with your willingness to work with me as we have done today."

"Like I had a choice," said Sydney, as the two doctors settled in to enjoy a drink together.

When his glass was empty, Gary packed his things and stood to leave. "You can let me know when our next session might fit into your agenda."

"My dear young man, Lois would be beyond upset with me for a month if I booked a date with you. She is the *only* person who is permitted to fill my schedule. You might suggest that we should meet again soon when you speak with her. Lois will then check my schedule and verify with me that in fact I do want to see you again. She is very protective of my time and I appreciate her so much."

"Sydney, I think we will make a great team."

Gary passed his business card to her. "We have miles to go, as I suspect you are aware. For now, I will take my leads from you. I might encourage you to change direction now and then if I feel we are 'stuck' in one area."

He hesitated, then said, "Can I ask if you are permitted to give me your business card, or do I ask Lois for that, too?"

Sydney pretended to push him out of her home. "Out. Get out!"

Truth be told, she felt sorry he was leaving.

35: Cabin #3 plays host

"Where are the chips?" Waine said. "Large bags. Eight of them. Carried them back from the big house myself."

Denis knew that Waine had a need to tell everyone what he brought. "Here you go, brother. I've got your chips right here. You put the box down just outside the door, on our *huge* balcony."

"Ah, that's correct. I did drop the box outside. Let me distribute them to our guests. This is our first party in our home since we moved here."

"I wouldn't necessarily count a 'bring your own everything' much of a party." Waine was patting his brother on the back as he spoke.

"You say this isn't much of a party," Denis said. "Have you looked outside? There's a mob out there, for Christ's sake. I would call this one hell of a party."

As the brothers joined the crowd they saw both Thomas and Paradise making their way over to cabin #3. Everyone gathered around them and, ever the protector of his family, Pops stepped forward.

"Paradise, Thomas, you must be bone tired. I've got cold water for you and we have every drink you can think of around here, so what's your pleasure?"

Never far from her husband, Eugenie spoke next. "Paradise, everyone here is so proud of you. We all liked Lenny, and we feel so sad that his cancer took him in such a short time. Most of us didn't even know Lenny had cancer. Shock all around the Cape."

Paradise had an idea so she stepped into the crowd to hug both Pops and Eugenie as she spoke. "Pops, can you find me one of those 'soap boxes' you always talk about people standing on to reach their audience? You've even stepped up on one a time or two, right?" Paradise was bone tired, but she needed this to unwind.

"No need, my love. Come with me." Thomas walked with Paradise up the steps and onto the tiny landing for cabin #3, and motioned for her to say a few words. Everyone gathered around the front of the cabin.

Paradise asked Thomas to get her a light beer, and while he did that she dove in.

"I am so thankful that the party continued after we kicked you out. I will say a few words and answer any questions, then I'm going to bed."

Timing was everything. Thomas handed Paradise her beer, gave her a kiss, and then turned to their friends and neighbours. "And I am staying to party with you and you and you. At least, that's my plan, although I might drop to the ground in an hour or two."

I may never get to speak, thought Paradise as she watched Eugenie make her way up the steps and over to her.

"My dear, I'm going to make sure every single person you see here leaves within the hour and goes home to bed."

"Stay up here with me," Paradise whispered to Eugenie. Giving her one more hug, she turned to face everyone.

"The saddest news is something you have heard already. Lenny is dead. He was diagnosed only months ago. Honestly, the trip all happened in a blur."

36: Chapter and verse

Paradise reached for her daughter's arm as she walked into the kitchen to grab a coffee. "Hope, honey, we keep passing each other like ships in the night these days," Paradise said. "Right now, right this minute, you and I are going to talk. Sit and talk to me."

"I'm good, mother."

"I'm not, Hope. I know you talked with Ben some-seventy-two hours ago, yet you haven't shared anything with me. I won't feel comfortable if he knocks on our door again and you and I have not talked. Are you still dating Ben, or are you officially single?"

"I'm officially sixteen, mom. Ben won't be knocking on my door anytime soon. I think that makes me 'single', if you need a word for it. Wait, you've been counting the hours since he was here? Really? I should have said something earlier. I know you and dad are very involved with Sydney and what happened during your last meeting with her, and I figured this could wait."

Hope was enjoying this conversation now that she had control of the narrative. "Ben told me all about the nearly-naked lady who I walked in on at his place, mom, but can we keep that discussion for when I'm ready, or older, or more mature, or smarter or whatever?"

Hope was surprised by her mom's response: "Sure."

She stifled a smile and continued. "I have to let his story grow on me before I can truly believe. We agreed we won't run away from each other, especially given the fact that we both live on Cape St

Mary Road. I asked Ben not to prance around here with his dates anytime soon, since I think I would still end up crying. He said he wouldn't be prancing for some time and I told him I appreciated that very much. And I meant it, mom."

Hope paused to take a bite of something she held in her hand. Paradise would ask about that later. For now she was not going to interrupt.

"I didn't say it to Ben, but I can't be bothered with how I feel about him (and I mean that in a good way...honestly I do) because I am going to spend all of my spare time learning about forensics. Did Sydney tell you she wants to help me determine how serious I am about this and how hard I am willing to work while I'm still in high school? She is going to send me a package in the mail. To be specific, it wasn't Sydney who told me any of this directly. She had Lois pass the information on to me, but, believe me, Lois can quote her boss chapter and verse. She is one loyal assistant. Mom, *she* has her own secretary. I was shocked to hear that, but for once I kept my mouth shut. Are you with me mom? Should I go on?"

"Please do," said Paradise.

"While I was with Lois, I learned so much from her during my tour of 'slab city', and I see you're ready to jump on me, but I swear the term came from Lois. She said working in the death industry, you have to make light of a few things to keep from being sad from morning until you go home at night. Or jaded, even; and, yes, I looked that word up after I heard Lois use it."

Paradise seemed to be stuck on something.

"Mom, are you okay? Did I lose you there for a second."

"Sorry, Hope. You didn't lose me at all, I promise. Your dad and I had a rough day with Sydney and I wanted both of us to fill you in. However, given all that *our* conversation is including at the moment, I'm going to give you a bit of background about what has happened with and to Sydney in the last week or two."

"You're frightening me, mom. Tell me now, *please.*"

Paradise decided to dive in. She would explain the circumstances to Thomas later, and knew he would understand. "Hope, there are only certain things I can share, because much of what we are working on is confidential between us and our client. This is good information for your Private Investigator training, though."

"Stop stalling, mom."

"Good catch, Hope. There is no right way to begin this story and it's difficult for me to put it into words but I'll try. Sydney has been attacked. There...I said it. It's the first time I have shared any of this."

Paradise took a second to have a sip of her coffee. "An intruder followed Sydney home and forced his way in as she unlocked her door."

"Mom, I really like Sydney. She isn't dying, is she?" Hope tried very hard to not cry.

"Well, she was attacked and beaten almost to death, but she is *not* going to die from it. She is not well enough to go to her offices, and will not be for some time. I believe Sydney wants to spare herself the looks of pity that will come her way. She isn't a woman who has ever wanted anyone to pity her."

Hope walked over to her mom and gave her a hug as they cried it out together. "I know there is so much more to Sydney's story, but I don't think I could digest any more of it right now."

"I'm relieved to hear it," said Paradise. "I don't think I could share any more details today."

"Mom, are we safe? Has this person been caught? Do you know for sure Sydney is safe? It would be so horrific if she had to face—"

"He's dead, Hope."

37: A cold and frosty sun

Bonde knew she had to get her shit together and go back to work, but first she had to clean her little apartment. "Have you not cleaned one corner of this place since Lenny died?" she asked herself,

She was tempted to call Jalen Lexis simply to interact with someone, but shook her head. "Pity party ends today."

A few hours later, when Bonde locked the door to her super-clean home, she made a point of leaving all the windows open. The breeze might help remove the smell of death that Bonde could still detect in her bed. At first she had loved it, but not so any more. She had actually bought all new bedding.

Bonde had lived alone for most of her life. Today she gave herself an imaginary smack up-side the head and turned her face to the sun.

Oh, how Lenny loved the sun on his face and body during his last few months on this earth, she thought. She wondered often if she would have felt so incredibly close to Lenny if he hadn't been dying when she invited him to move in. *Who am I kidding? In a healthy body, Lenny wouldn't have given me the time of day*. They worked together at 2.0. End of story...until it wasn't.

Without Lenny, Bonde felt the sun turn against her. She could almost feel a cool frostiness from the sun. What was that about?

Letting her mind go back to Jalen, Bonde couldn't help but feel guilty that she was still at home and hadn't even checked in. He called her daily for the first week, when all the paperwork related to Lenny's passing was being completed. He had been so incredibly generous in paying both Bonde and Lenny their full salaries and packaging it as if they were doing *him* a favour.

Bonde needed a plan and decided the frosty sunshine was not her friend today, and she would try another day.

Yes, Lieutenant Commander Jalen Lexis had turned out to be so many good things wrapped up into a very sexy package. Bonde noticed that, since Lenny's passing, Jalen had been rather cool towards her, perhaps out of respect for Lenny. She wanted to talk to him about that, because when she returned to work, she planned to be her 'I am Woman, Hear Me Roar' self.

She was anxious to learn whom she would be working with on the night shift. Maybe she could take the shift on by herself and get a bit of a pay raise to go along with that.

Bonde picked up the pace en route home from the beautiful beach that kisses the ocean along Kalakawa Avenue. She collected her mail at the door and turned the key in her bright red door, thanks to Lenny.

She found her feet were talking her straight to the phone.

Some things never change...he still picks up on the first ring. Like there is a fire somewhere or a woman is giving birth on the warehouse floor. Or worse, a woman is flirting with him and he can't take it...not on the job!

"Lieutenant Commander Jalen Lexis. Identify yourself."

"I had actually forgotten how your straight-laced Hawaii 5.0 training sounds. I think I have missed that about you, sir. How is that even possible?"

Jalen heard her chuckle and hoped that was an indication that she was dealing with Lenny's death and learning to grieve at her own pace.

"Bonde, how are you? I have been hoping you would call. I didn't want to overwhelm you with daily checking on you, which often resulted in silence...neither of us knowing just what to say, or how we wanted to say it."

"Sir, and I *am* calling you 'sir', because I like the way it rolls around in my mouth. And there you have it, ladies and gentlemen: the dead silence we spoke of. But seriously, sir, we need to talk about me returning to work. I don't want you to feel I have taken you for granted. I appreciate every dollar you have paid me and I'm wondering if we could talk about combining both my and Lenny's job with a bit of a pay raise at some point. I think I would be safe there by myself on the night shift. Lord knows we didn't have even one attempted intruder during the many long nights Lenny and I worked together."

"We can talk about it, but it's never going to happen. I would never leave you alone in the warehouse all night."

"Careful, sir: I smell a 'little woman' story and you know how I hate stories about protecting the wee women in our tribe."

"Bonde, let me buy you dinner. We'll go somewhere, anywhere that you and Lenny didn't go to, because, while you and I both loved Lenny, I want to talk with you about a few things career-wise."

"Sir, I will have dinner with you anytime, anywhere, as long as you don't bring any of that 'dead silence' that happens between us. It's rare that I am at a loss for words, as you well know, so it must be you, not me, who comes with pockets full of dead silence."

Jalen couldn't help but smile, listening to her go on and on and on."What about tomorrow evening? I'll pick you up around 8:30."

"What about tonight? I'll be ready at 7:30."

Bonde couldn't believe she was being so bold with Jalen. It was one thing to flirt with him in the warehouse, but this was out in the open. This was personal. It was lovely that they could spend time with each other in their time of grief. They would grieve differently, of course, because no two people grieve exactly the same.

Bonde decided she would hang up on the man because; well, because there was that damn dead silence again. She would just assume he would pick her up at 7:30.

She would be right. Bonde was outside watching for her 'date' and, sure enough, as the clock approached exactly the time *she* had suggested, Jalen pulled into her driveway and gave her his beautiful smile the second he saw her.

38: Checking in on Sydney

Paradise and Thomas knew they wouldn't turn their back on Sydney, not now, not ever. She had become a friend, at least with Paradise. Additionally, after a rough start on the phone with Hope, Sydney had come to like the young teenager very much. Paradise wondered if Hope might remind Sydney of someone else.

"Paradise, do me a favour, sweetheart," Thomas said. "Please call Lois to see what she thinks of you coming into the city to speak with Sydney. Your friendship, rather than your PI experience, could get you in the door. But there is no point making the trip if Sydney will not even see you."

Hearing Hope come out of her room and down the stairs, Paradise said, "Good morning, Hope. Grab the phone on your way to the kitchen, where your dad is pouring your coffee at this very second...Thank you, honey."

Hope handed the phone to her mom with one hand and with the other took a large black coffee from her dad.

Hope was always welcome to join her parents at the kitchen table, so she assumed today was no exception. "I couldn't hear your discussion from my bedroom, as you both know, but I could tell it was serious. Nothing worse has happened to Sydney I hope?" Hope had grown very fond of Sydney and was in awe of her line of work.

"You have such a kind heart, Hope. Don't ever change." Paradise reached over to give her girl a sideways-hug. They just happened to be sitting on the same side of the table.

Jumping into the conversation. Thomas said, “Your mom is anxious to visit Sydney to see what we can do to help her. We need her to know we come as friends, not as PIs.”

“Or, PIs’ daughter,” Hope offered with a smile.

“If you two can keep it down a bit, why don’t I call Lois from right here? I won’t put her on speakerphone, but at least you will hear my side of things. This might save us time when I hang up.”

Paradise could see that Hope had something to say. “What is it, Hope?”

Hope realized she had annoyed her mother, but decided she would ask anyway. “Please, can I go, too? *Please?*

“No.”

“No,” Thomas said at the same time.

“‘A ‘no’ from one of you would have been sufficient. Mom, let’s make that call.”

Paradise reached Lois at the second number Lois had given her. “Lois, it’s Paradise. Am I interrupting you? Are you with Sydney? Her blood pressure might go sky-high if she knows it’s me, so I will leave that to your judgment. Sorry, Lois, that was a long-winded way to ask if I was catching you at a good time.”

Only when she stopped talking did Paradise realize she was nervous. A friend at the Cape police station had told her that when she was nervous she suffered from verbal-diarrhea. She should have thought of that before making the call.

They heard muffled sounds at the other end of the conversation, then Lois said, “I’ll call you back. Please stand by.”

Paradise handed the phone to Hope. “When she calls back, why don’t you answer? But then hand the phone over to me after just a minute or two.”

“Thanks, mom!”

After seven long minutes the phone in Hope’s hand rang.

"Oh my God, Lois it's me. It's Hope. Mom and dad told me what happened to Sydney. How is she today? I promise to ask how you are in a second or two. I only have two minutes before I hand the phone to mom so talk fast."

There was a bit of silence, but as Hope was gearing up to ask a couple more questions, she heard Lois take a deep breath.

Except it wasn't Lois.

"Hello, Hope. I hate to disappoint you, but I asked Lois to make the call then hand the phone over to me. How are you, dear? Lois tells me you asked a million questions when you were with her in our offices. In my world, that indicates someone is keenly interested in the topic. Death and dying aren't for party conversations, trust me."

Sydney was delighted to have something positive to think of, at least for a second or two. She admired Hope's spunk.

"Doctor Scott, Sydney, I am sorry I didn't know it was you calling. Does this remind you of the first time we spoke when you were calling mom and I answered and had a million questions about why anyone who works with dead people would be calling mom? Oh, no, mom's making that 'wrap it up' motion, so talk fast, how are you?"

Hope saw her mother's extended hand so she turned the phone over, as she had promised.

"Sydney, it's Paradise. Please consider this a call from a friend. A friend who would love to come and visit you just to catch up on anything and everything."

"Paradise, why don't you come for lunch tomorrow? And bring your inquisitive daughter along with you. Lois was impressed with the questions Hope had for her and she will be here tomorrow, too. I'll have her join us for lunch, and after lunch we will leave Hope with Lois and you and I can talk business."

After thinking for a second, Sydney spoke again, but on an entirely different topic. "I don't give apologies over the phone or in print. I believe if you have to offer an apology, you should make it in person when you can look the person in the eye. I'll be doing that tomorrow."

"How does 11:30 tomorrow morning work for you, Sydney? And Hope is already very excited about seeing you and Lois again."

"That sounds perfect. See you then."

With that Sydney hung up. For the first time in a while she had a smile on her face.

39: Friendships

Surprised to see Sydney in the open doorway of her Halifax home, smiling as she waved, Paradise was the first to speak. "Sydney, you don't look any better today and—"

Hope interrupted. "Sydney, what did he do to you? Is there a way I can help you? I'll do anything for you."

She ran to Sydney and wrapped her arms around her.

Sydney tried to hold back because she didn't want to alarm Hope. After a second or less she cried out in pain, "Hope, my ribs are broken and so is the arm you are leaning on dear, so get off me, please."

"Did I make your injuries worse? Oh. My. God, mom, I wouldn't blame you if you locked me in the car while you visit with Sydney."

Hope was bordering on hysteria and both Sydney and Paradise were stunned by her outburst.

Sydney tried to make light of the situation. "Dear Lord, I am in such pain. Lois, could you bring me a pain reliever and some water to wash it down?"

She and her visitors stood in an awkward silence in the doorway until Lois had returned with Sydney's medication.

"Lois, thank you, dear, I feel better already."

Sydney gulped the pill with a bit too much water. Pretending there was no one else in the room, she wiped off droplets that had landed on her neck and her blouse...and her slacks, too, she realized.

With obvious pain Sydney turned to her two guests. "I have not always seemed to be 'myself' these last few days, but, Hope, I'm relatively certain you don't have to be locked in the car simply because you gave me a hug. However, I swear you broke the only intact rib I had left, so if you so much as touch me I will scream again. And then I will ponder that look of absolute fright you wore on your entire face as you heard me scream a few minutes ago. Was it that bad, truly? Should I demonstrate that scream, or perhaps I should remember my manners instead and invite you both in. Paradise, please take Hope into the living room and I will see how our lunch is coming along. Unfortunately I can't yet sit at my own dining room table, but I think we can eat with lunch on our laps since I have ordered pretty much all finger food. The only way I can manage to eat on my own at the moment is if I am able to pick my food up with my one operable hand and deposit each piece directly into my mouth."

Sydney stepped out of Hope's way with a bit of fanfare, and motioned for both ladies to come on in.

Allowing herself time before she returned to her guests, Sydney said to Lois in a hushed tone, "Pain is not going away, Lois. I swear to God it felt like something else broke when Hope hugged me. What do you think I could do to make myself even a bit more comfortable while my guests are here? They drove over three hours for this lunch."

"Yes, yes I know how long they were on the road, but I don't give a rat's ass about either of them," Lois whispered back. I'm going to call your doctor and see if he thinks you should come in for an x-ray immediately. If I was in your position right now I would tell my guests that I had fallen ill and will have to reschedule."

Lois thought she might be a bit jealous of Paradise and Hope. They seemed to make her boss a million times happier than she had ever been able to."You do remember Doctor Langille is coming later this afternoon...and staying for dinner." Why does he get to spend the evening meal with you all the time? You know I love having dinner with you."

So, I am jealous, Lois finally admitted to herself.

"Difference is that Gary is my shrink and he can take a look at my pain relief schedule and bring me a magic pill that will give me a few hours free of pain. Tell Gary that. I'm not looking for a total change in my meds delivered by my shrink who is only supposed to be my 'head' guy, that is to say he need concern himself only with what I'm thinking and how my overall mental health is on any given day. I just want an extra pain relief pill and he gets to choose the pill, but not preach to me about pain management. Make sure he knows I asked you to tell him that. If you must, tell him a teenager tackled me and broke yet another rib."

With that, Sydney turned to go to her guests, but as she was half in and half out of the room, she said, "Oh, one more thing, Lois."

"Yes, Colombo," replied Lois. They shared a love for the television series featuring the dishevelled Lieutenant Colombo. He rarely left a scene without stopping just short of the door, when he would turn, point a finger and say, 'There is one more thing. Just something I'm trying to figure out.'

Using what they had come to call their 'Colombo pose' Sydney pointed a finger and said, "Ask...no, *tell* Gary to cancel the rest of his appointments for the day so he can bring me something *now.*"

Lois wasn't sure this was wise, but Colombo often charged forward and that's what her boss was about to do.

"I apologize, ladies. I had a few things to review with Lois. I never have much going on in my house unless it involves doctors and nurses needing to 'look at me' to see how I'm healing. Some of them hover, but I try to understand all of this from their perch. Some have gone from never meeting me in all the years they have worked on my team to seeing more of me than they want to. I had to talk with some of them about the look of pity they offer while we are talking. I do have pity parties, but I'll damn well have them by myself."

Hope was confused. "I don't know what you mean by a look of pity or a perch or something like that."

Sydney said, "Hope, when you tried to tackle me, that was you showing that you care about me. I believe your exact words were, 'Sydney what did he do to you?' Now, let me demonstrate the look of pity to you. I'll stand right in front of you. Hope, we need a reason for me to show pity, just to make it more real, so let me assume you have a really nice boyfriend and then I hear you have broken up...I see you at a coffee shop, so I approach you immediately, lower my head, tilt it like this, and, in my low-slow-pity voice, I say, 'Ohhhhh, Hope. I heard about your breakup with the hunk and I am *so* sorry. You must be devastated. I hope you are doing okay? Should I sit here beside you or do you want to grieve alone? I'll be in touch because we will have to get you *out there* again. Gotta run.'"

Paradise was laughing out loud. "If that was your best acting, Sydney, I suggest you never give up your day job. However, I will say the combination of the lower voice and the tilt of the head was genius. Have you done this before?"

Paradise laughed again, and this time Sydney and Hope joined in.

40: Humble pie

"Doctor Scott," said the lady in a maid's costume, "may I serve lunch? I can wheel in a table with everything set up for you. You and your guests can help yourselves and I will be in the kitchen if you need me."

No introduction of the lady seemed awkward, and rude, to Hope, but she kept her mouth shut while giving her mother one of her best '*What the?'* looks.

Not long after the ladies began eating, Paradise was full and admitted it. She thanked Sydney for letting her and Hope visit with her. "Given how we left things last time Thomas and I were here, I am so appreciative of you sharing your time today."

"Hope, Paradise, you will notice there is no dessert on the table. That's because I am personally serving *Humble Pie* for you, Paradise, and for Thomas, even though I didn't invite him to join us. I don't know why I said what I said, but it is not the fault of my broken bones, broken ribs or my surgeries. It's all on me. I was so far out of line, it's a wonder I didn't fall over. I am so very sorry, and I can only hope you will find it in your hearts to forgive me."

"Say no more. All is forgiven," said Paradise.

Sydney whispered and seemed on the verge of tears, "Thank you. Thank you."

Almost as if on cue, Lois appeared. "Sydney, I have the literature you pulled for Hope to take home. I have printed it in duplicate so Paradise will have the same details that her daughter has. Your directions are on the last page stating that Hope is to take her time to review and digest *all* documents before your next meeting." Lois motioned for Hope to follow her.

"You will be in the family room, correct, Lois? We will give you a shout when your mom is ready to head home, Hope."

Paradise added, looking directly at her daughter, "Hope, this is the business part of our trip that I reviewed briefly with you, remember?'

"Yes, mother, of course I remember. That was only a couple of hours ago. I am not to interrupt you and Sydney. I am not to make a noise of any kind. I am not to break anything while we're here. Really, mother, I do remember."

Paradise made a mental note to talk with Hope about that little performance.

As soon as the girls were gone, Paradise had a question she couldn't hold for another second. "Honestly, Sydney, how much did Hope hurt you with that bear hug she gave you?"

"Honestly? On a scale of 1 to 10 the pain was, and is, a hard 10. Lois gave me something for the added pain before we started and my shrink is supposed to bring something more effective and fast acting when he comes for my session. How lucky am I that my shrink comes to me? I'm not always like this, as I think you know. Broken ribs are the worst. I swear if I sneeze, I cry with the pain from the involuntary body reflex."

"How does your doctor feel about you calling him a shrink?"

"I'll call him worse than a shrink if he doesn't get here soon. I asked Lois to see if he could come earlier, like five minutes ago."

"Sydney, in case he does get here soon, can we deal with a few things? First and foremost, are Thomas and I *not* fired?"

"Correct. Next?"

"We have worked around the clock, trying to find out why a child molester was let out of jail pending his trial and we have no answers yet. No one knew his plan was to come here to your home, Sydney. We are 100% sure of that. Did he already know where you live? We don't have that answer, either. And, surprisingly, no one, not even his criminal lawyer, seems to know he is dead. In his world, I suspect no one cares about whether he is dead or alive."

"Next?"

"We both want you to know how terrible we feel that this happened. My God, that horrible criminal could have shot and killed you. Thomas and I have given other PIs or local policemen our entire workload for the month, so we are working on this 24/7."

"Point taken. Next?"

Paradise looked around to ensure no one was lurking. "Sydney, what about...you know...the person you asked me to devote my time to once this trial was over—and, of course, now it's over before it began. Should I start working on this file now, and what name can we give the file?"

"Thank you for bringing this up. This is all I really wanted to talk about today, but then I invited Hope...."

Both ladies smiled before Sydney continued. "The second I recognized his voice and he removed the ski mask I asked him about my child. He was quick to correct me with, 'I believe you mean *our* child.' He only offered nuggets of hope and I need to see what I can remember that might be helpful to you and Thomas."

"Could your shrink help you with this at all?"

"Yes, he will. However, he doesn't know yet."

"Keeping secrets from me, are you, Doctor Scott?"

Both women turned to face the man standing in the doorway.

Sydney was agitated. "Gary, how long have you been listening in on our conversation? How dare you? I can't believe you would do that to me."

Gary was surprised by her outburst and his words were evidence of this. "*Doctor Scott,* I stopped in the kitchen to get water so you could take the pill you asked that I bring to you as soon as possible. All I heard as I walked from there to here was, 'He doesn't know yet.' Not for a second did I think it was me you were talking about, Sydney. I was being a wise guy, and that wasn't all that wise, as it turns out. Do you still have the extra pain and do you want this pill or not? I have an urgent case, youth attempted suicide, and I only give you that detail because I know you might make the accusation that I'm cancelling because of what I heard spoken in this room. I didn't think anyone else should bring you extra meds, so here you are. I must run."

Gary placed the pill in Sydney's hand but refused to move his hand away until she looked up at him. "As always, I will call Lois to schedule our next appointment. Everything is as *you* like it to be. Sydney, understand this...I did not rush over because you demanded I do so. I rushed first to your lead doctor to find out what medication I could write a script for and then I rushed over *because I care about you.*"

Not lowering his voice, as he left the room, the shrink added, "And whoever your guest is, perhaps you might introduce us next time we are all in the same room and you are firing accusations at me."

With that Doctor Gary Langille left as he had come in...through the side door, the only door where the help was allowed to enter the house.

Speaking to the inside of his car while it warmed up, Gary ended today's 'Doctor Scott' tape with, "Sydney, I think you're ready for a bit of tough love when we next meet and that won't be any day soon. You have some homework to do, and only you can figure out what that homework looks like. Don't let me down doctor. You've got this."

41: Leftovers

Paradise thought she would be the first into the kitchen. She had promised Hope, who was still in bed, that she would be right back with coffee.

Muffled sounds as she locked the door made Paradise smile. Hope was clearly enjoying the offer of coffee via room-service-by-mother. "Hurry back with my coffee, mother, please!"

Sydney was so frightened to hear footsteps behind her that she jumped, which of course made every single bruise, surgery repair, and broken bone hurt like hell.

'Snot-crying,' as she would later call it, Sydney was happy to see a familiar face. "Paradise, you are a strong woman. Thanks for catching me...just after you nearly scared me to death."

"Just yesterday Hope almost wrestled you to the ground. And now I frighten you and may have caused you to break any bones not yet broken. I bet you can't wait to see the back of my car with us both heading out of town."

Paradise could see that Sydney was shaken up. "Let me take a coffee to my caffeine-dependent daughter before she comes looking for me. Then maybe we could sit and have our coffee together."

Sydney was quick to reply. "I would like that. Lois is working from our offices today and, given that my kitchen queen has taught me how to make coffee, we will have total privacy. As you probably realize, the real reason I asked you and Hope to bunk in here with me was that I didn't think we would have time to fully discuss what

I am wrestling with. Some days I am so weak by 6 pm I literally go to bed and sleep until morning. Everyone tells me I have to rest when my body tells me to, but the word 'lazy' comes to mind also."

"Okay, Sydney, this is me taking Hope a coffee and one of those warm muffins I spotted. If you want to pour my coffee, I will be back in seconds and we can work until you get too tired." With that Paradise was rushing down the hall.

After waking Hope up (again) Paradise asked her to call Thomas to let him know they wouldn't be home until late afternoon. "Tell him Sydney wants to continue with us as her private investigators. Your dad will know what I'm talking about."

"Does it matter that *I* don't know what you're talking about?"

"I will tell you what I can en route home later today. It's imperative you give us total privacy for three hours. Use that time to start reviewing the material that Sydney gave you. We will also be discussing this *ask* of Sydney during our windshield time."

With that Paradise turned and ran back down the hallway to meet with her client.

"Oh good, you're back. Here's your coffee but let me have the floor for a minute. I don't believe I can talk about this twice, once with you and once with my shrink, so he is joining us any minute. That's okay with you right?"

"Assuming I know what 'this' is, of course I'm totally fine with whatever makes *you* comfortable. And I will be calling him Doctor Langille, not your shrink."

Paradise took a seat at the kitchen table only to be reminded that Sydney's broken bones etc didn't allow her to sit comfortably in her own kitchen.

"Follow me, please, I have three spots all arranged...with my good arm only I will add."

Leading the way Sydney added, "I want both of you in front of me so my neck doesn't have to work too hard. I've been having neck pains for a couple of days, but my medical doctor will be here later today. I swear I have the most wonderful team, and it seems they drop in either en route to work or en route home at night. It's about time for me to put a stop to that. I still need help with so much of my recovery it's good to know so many doctors are on my team and by my side."

They entered the living room, and Paradise waited for Sydney to sit before choosing one of the other prepared places.

"Sydney, should I assume Doctor Langille is your psychologist, and nothing more than that? Your relationship seemed more personal yesterday than I had assumed it would be."

"Early days, Paradise, and that's all I will say on the subject. I have never in my life dated anyone, for reasons that you know. I'm not sure I ever will." Sydney seemed sad, and her last statement was left hanging in mid air.

As if on cue a deep voice came from somewhere between the side entrance and the kitchen. "Shrink entering the side entrance, and will report for duty in three seconds. Good morning, ladies. Is this coffee for me, Sydney?"

Without waiting for a reply, Doctor Langille took a sip of his coffee.

"Why aren't you sitting down, Gary? Are you not staying?" Sydney seemed angry.

"Because I know you have impeccable manners and will want to introduce me to this other lady."

Paradise stood and reached out to shake Gary's hand. "Doctor Langille, I'm Paradise d'Entremont from down the line, Clare region, to be specific. I'm Sydney's personal private investigator and have been for some time. I will let her take it from there."

Paradise sat and smiled at Sydney, who gave her a nod.

"And, as you have clearly heard, I'm Sydney's shrink." He too was smiling at Sydney.

""Gary," Sydney said, "I have saved one slice of humble pie for you. I will never call you my shrink again. In fact, I won't use that expression again for any reason. I treated you poorly by demanding you come to me yesterday, and I hope you will accept my humble apology."

"Apology accepted. No harm done." Gary added with a chuckle, "Was I wrong in thinking this was a breakfast meeting, given the ungodly early hour?"

Paradise jumped up, seeing this as a perfect time to give the two doctors a minute or two of alone time. "I happen to know where the pantry is and I can tell you it's loaded with anything you might like."

"I know the pantry here always stocks muffins, and that would be all I need, Paradise, thank you. I am not a good morning person, nor do I eat much with my first few cups of coffee."

"The mother in me wants to say you really must start eating breakfast, Gary, but that might be for another day."

Paradise was off in search of breakfast for four. She would drop a plate off for Hope before rejoining the meeting.

Gary could see Sydney wanted the floor so he sat and remained quiet with both hands around his almost empty coffee cup.

"Gary, please know I'm sincerely sorry for my behaviour yesterday."

That seemed to Gary to be the easy part of what Sydney wanted to say and he was right. There was more. Much more.

Eventually, Paradise slipped quietly back into the room. She brought with her a tray with an assortment of fresh fruit, muffins, and croissants with fruit of some sort that looked too good to leave in the pantry. She also brought a fresh pot of coffee.

Sydney needed to stand for a bit because her healing bones were telling her to do so. This gave her a second or two to collect her thoughts.

Then she turned to her guests. "I will tell my story to you both as I don't think I could share this more than once in my current condition. What Paradise knows and you do not might startle you. I will do my best to bring you both up to date."

Paradise motioned that she would refill coffee cups.

42: Beginning at the end

Sydney took a deep breath before she began sharing her deepest, darkest secret. "I've decided to begin at the end of my story. As impossible as this is to believe, the monster I murdered a few days ago was the same man who raped and impregnated me when I was a child. You have no idea how tough it is for me to share this with you or anyone else." Sydney realized she was crying, so she explained she would likely cry much of the time.

"Gary, part of this story is not news to Paradise. While they were doing research on this monster's history, both Paradise and Thomas understood that finding and tracking him would not be the end of their contract with me. As a coroner I have completed autopsies on too many young women, girls really, from the Valley and have noted in my records that police needed this information. The particular similarity of the double break of one arm needed to be investigated. I remember thinking a monster might be lurking around young children and that he needed to be caught. Who would believe that he murdered all of the women he raped, excluding his first and his last victim? The young girl all those years ago *and* his last victim of a few days ago are one and the same person. That one surviving victim is me. *Me*."

She took a shuddering breath. "My tank is empty at the moment. Paradise, why don't you review what the next part of your contract with me will include and then we will get you and Hope on the road to Thomas and Lee. Gary, after Paradise leaves you and I can discuss what your role will be in terms of my mental health. I know I have work to do going back to my childhood memories, and if that's not part of your pay-grade you can refer me to another shrink...I'm not calling *you* that, of course."

Paradise was on her feet. "Sydney, I can certainly try to make this quick. Correct me if I misspeak or misquote you or others."

Turning to Gary, Paradise said, "I am on contract to find and contact the child born to this monster and Sydney some years ago. Sydney heard her newborn baby cry. She knew her child was alive. Her baby was still crying as he or she was taken from the birthing room. No one would even tell Sydney if her child was a baby boy or baby girl. Sydney was made to get up off the birthing table, help clean the room, and then leave the hospital. They kicked her out just hours after she had given birth. She walked back to the unwed-mothers' boarding house where she had lived for seven long months thanks to her own mother who shipped her off to 'her aunt's house', as it was explained to her friends and church-going peers. Sydney's parents moved out of state and made sure she couldn't find them when she came 'crawling back home' following the birth of the child. The last words Sydney said to her mother were, 'I haven't crawled since I was nine months old, mother. If you don't want me here, don't you worry, I won't come home. I won't be crawling back to you or to anyone else.'"

"Paradise," Sydney said, "you began by saying you could make this quick. I would hate to hear your long version. I am shocked to hear you quote me word for word. You're a walking tape-recorder. You have much more to offer, if and when you have been a private investigator long enough and want to spread your wings. We can talk about this another time. I'm sorry, now I'm the one taking too long."

Turning to Gary, Sydney asked if he wanted to stand up for a minute just to stretch or walk around but he quickly said he was okay for now. What he didn't say was that he *did not* want to break the momentum of what was happening in the moment.

"Back to me, people!" Paradise said in her outside voice. "I will wrap up by saying I will be in touch with you, dear Sydney. And Doctor Langille, I know my friend is going to be in good hands with you. It's a pleasure to know you. I'm off to pick up my girl and get on the road. If we make good time we can put our toes into the ocean at Mavillette beach before Lee has to go to bed. I'll show myself out...you two have work to do."

As she reached the door Paradise turned and said, "Oh, there is one small thing I forgot to ask—"

Sydney cut her off mid sentence. "So...who's Columbo now?"

Belly laughs all around.

"Seriously Paradise, what could you possibly have forgotten?"

"Money! We have bills to pay. Do I correctly assume we are able to bill you once again?"

"Absolutely, and I want to say that, only seconds after I fired you, I asked Lois to track your hours and make sure we pay you accurately and on time up to and including today. I don't want any we-pity-you-so-we-will-lower-our-rate story, now go before I kick you out."

Sydney slowly got up from her chair to give the smallest of hugs to Paradise. Gary could hear her whispering to Paradise, but he couldn't make out what she was saying.

43: The long way home

"Hope," Paradise said, "you have been such a great side-kick for me on this trip and, in particular, you're not even upset that you had to spend this entire sunny morning in our room because of the privacy Sydney needed for our morning discussion. Sydney has given me permission to share our discussion with you, but only if you want to hear it."

She reached over and gave her girl a fast sideways hug.

Hope was quick with her own version of her morning spent stuck inside a room big enough to house a family of four. "Mom, I have to say spending half the day sleeping in, a *second* cup of coffee with breakfast served in bed by my very own waitress/mother, plus a television all to myself, all added up to be a win for me. Poor me, right, mom?"

"Seriously, you adapt very well for a teenager, Hope. We stayed overnight, which had not been in the original plans at all, and you didn't so much as whimper about plans with friends at home that you would have to cancel. You know what I mean. I want you to know you can travel with me anytime. Now, a change of pace for our next windshield topic. You get to pick a *different* topic for our next discussion. Take us back to Cape St Mary Road and tell me what your 16-year-old mind sees happening in our little corner of the world. Not in general terms, but what *you* see."

Paradise knew she would need to be ready for anything, and Hope did not disappoint.

"Mom, talk to me about you and dad, please. I know the basics, but I wish you could tell me how you knew at such a young age that dad was the one."

"First time, as you know I did *not* pick dad. I picked God. I entered the convent the night before my 16th birthday. Your father looked at me with utter contempt, disappointment and sadness as I tried to explain my total devotion to the Catholic Church. I didn't realize I was pregnant when I entered the convent. I didn't know that your dad adopted you and moved to Honolulu. I didn't know that I would leave the convent and move back to my home community after five years. I didn't know that I would eventually become a private investigator."

"Mom. Mom. Mom. I pretty much know all of this, but when you stepped off the plane the first time we met I saw lots of love in your eyes for me. My dad, not so much. Why was that? You're not telling me what I need to know, though. *How did you know?"*

"Shock. Surprise. Confusion when you stepped out from behind your dad. I will forever cherish the memory of you being shy as you asked, 'Do you know who I am? Do you think we look alike? I think we do look a lot like each other but do you?' Hope, I thought my heart would burst when I laid eyes on you."

Paradise paused, but just long enough to swallow a tear or two.

"How much of this is about Ben, sweetheart? Don't answer that yet, but let me continue. You dad and I were just short of frantic when you and Ben stepped onto the dance floor during our wedding celebration. Tall, dark and handsome and no one knew who he was. You were exactly the same age that I was when I realized I was pregnant with you and—"

"Mom, sorry to interrupt, but I want to assure you that there is no 'Ben and I' and I mean that. Ben understands that I have accepted his offer to pick me up for my graduation formal dance. I'm only in grade ten, mom, so you've got a few years to *not* worry, I promise you that. One day I would like to have a relationship like the one you and dad have. Before I find my husband, I have so much to do. Lois told me that Sydney hopes to mentor me when I head to university. I told her I wanted to be a forensic scientist. I told her via Lois, and Lois thought that was very interesting because I had almost fainted when she took me to the morgue and showed me one poor sod who was awaiting his autopsy. There I am in the morgue almost puking and Lois didn't skip a beat. She kept talking, and when I rebounded and asked a few questions she told me she was impressed. Mom, the dead people are all in coolers along the wall on slabs where they await their fate. Lois opened the first door and didn't even prepare me. It's funny now, but not then. She told me they have no identification for this man, so what will happen to his body is unknown. He was homeless, lived on the street and no one had claimed the body. Isn't that sad?"

"Yes, the experience you have had is remarkable. I'm glad that your mind is on your education and not boys at the moment. Now: change of topic, because I think we should stop at a restaurant that has a pay phone. We will call the boys collect and see if we can bring them supper. Sound good?"

"Sure." Hope was reverting back to her one-word responses and it was just what was needed to lighten the mood in the car.

"Mom, I hope I didn't tell you too much about the morgue and the dead people. I just wanted to make sure you understand my mind is well occupied and not fixated on the lovely Ben."

"I'm not sure a 16-year-old girl can ever tell her mother too much, dear. I do want to tell you that we say deceased rather than dead people. Just a bit of vocabulary upgrade for your next time in the morgue."

Paradise was starving so they pulled off the main highway in pursuit of fine food to go.

"Deceased bodies or just deceased?" Hope loved learning little things from her mom.

"Deceased."

"Roger that," said Hope.

Both mother and daughter had already moved on to thoughts of food.

44: Yet another Cape party

Hope was getting concerned. Her mother had been on the restaurant payphone for a very long time. All she had to do was get Lee and her dad's supper order.

"Can I help you, young lady?"

Hope was sitting at a table, but she wouldn't know what the plan was until her mom stopped talking. And she sure hadn't seen the waitress heading her way until she spoke.

"Oh, maybe I shouldn't sit down yet? My mom is on the phone checking to see if our family wants us to arrive home with dinner for four or just for the two of us. I didn't get the table dirty, I promise. I'll just go and see why she is taking so long."

"You sit right here and I will bring you some water. Then you can just relax and wet your whistle."

"Can I just tell you that meeting folks like you is the reason I actually like living in Nova Scotia more than I liked living in Honolulu?"

When her waitress returned with her glass of water, Hope started comparing the Cape in Nova Scotia to Hawaii. After seven or eight 'for example's, the waitress said, "Oh, my dear, there are so many degrees of *wrong* in those statements young lady. But I'm glad you chose to live here and I'm glad you picked my restaurant to dine in or to take out. Totally your choice."

"I hope I'm not taking up too much of your time with my rambling."

"You're not rambling at all, and you can sit here as long as it takes. I'm going to rustle up some grub for you. I won't be a minute."

Hope stood up and extended her hand. "I'm Hope, by the way. My mother's name is Paradise."

But her waitress had already turned and gone through the swinging doors to what Hope assumed was the kitchen.

"Is someone calling my name? Sorry to take so long, sweetheart."

Paradise came rushing back to the table just as the waitress appeared with a huge plate of French fries. "Hope, I see we have ordered? These fries smell like heaven."

"They're on the house, and you'll love 'em. Everybody does. Your delightful daughter has been keeping me company. Scoot over, honey. I'm inviting myself to join you for a minute, or for as long as it takes for another customer to walk in. Now, what will it be, Paradise: take out for four or this table for the two of you?"

Smiling as she turned to her daughter Paradise said, "Neither, believe it or not. More often than not, when we are away from our home for even one night, there seems to be a Cape party at *our* place when we get back. And, when I tell you *everyone* in the Cape is invited, that's no exaggeration."

"Mom, that's not a bad thing. Remember how we shut everyone down, or sent them all to Cabin #3, when we came back from Honolulu? This could be a nice way to thank everyone for planning that party for us, even though we were the only ones who elected to not attend."

"Oh, the party is on," said Paradise. "You dad wanted to review *everyone* invited and I was in charge of listening to ensure he didn't forget anyone. Every other minute Lee had to interrupt to tell me one more thing his young mind had to share. Again, I apologize for taking so long."

"I might be going to a party tonight then! I'm Adelia, same name as you saw on the outside of my restaurant. Now what are we going to feed what sounds like the entire population of the Cape?"

"Oh. My. God. Are we taking up your time when you probably would be closed by now since you have a party to go to?" Turning to her mom, Hope said, "Let's let Adelia close up."

Adelia spoke through her laughter. "I just invited myself to the same party you're going to. I'm not a shy person. You can't be shy in this business. What will you be serving, or will everyone bring their own food and drink, as I know they often do in the Cape?"

"You're not from the Cape by chance?" Hope asked. "Oh. My. God. Mom, this is fate. I can feel it in my bones."

Turning back to Adelia, Hope asked, "You are from the Cape, right? Do you live in Cape St Mary? Have we seen you before?"

"Whoa there, Nellie. Hope, bring your mom and follow me into the kitchen and we can talk while I work. I've got an idea about the snacks you could take home. How many people will be in attendance? How hungry—I mean, will they have eaten before coming to your party? Finger foods okay? Plates and utensils can get ugly, so we need lots of napkins instead."

Paradise and Hope were feeling out of their element standing by in the kitchen after they answered all of her questions. They kept hoping Adelia would share her plans for this food. They hadn't discussed cost and money was very scarce at the moment.

"Ladies, I haven't been to a Cape party in a long time. Give me your address and I will deliver an array of whatever's left in my kitchen today. This will be my gift, and no arguments. Address, please."

Hope had a feeling and she was about to get some answers. "Adelia, we live at 548 Cape St Mary Road."

A large platter fell from Adelia's hands to the floor with an ear-deafening thud. She turned to them and said, "My grandparents grew up in 548 long before it was bulldozed and replaced with a modern home with no care or attention to the original design…just my opinion but that's for another discussion. For now, we feed the party-goers at 548. You girls go home and explain why you've arrived empty handed. Tonight's snacks will come with a caterer who is also the server."

Swinging a rather large knife in her hand, Adelia added, "Go. Go. Go. I will be thirty minutes behind you…forty, at the most. I want to lock the door behind you. I'm headed for a trip down memory lane and tonight I have no time to serve other customers."

Stunned silence from both mother and daughter when they returned to their car and got back on the road heading for home.

Paradise finally spoke. "At some point this evening, let's find our own private corner in the house, with a quiet vibe, if possible. We can have the same discussion we would have had during our 'windshield time', but tonight we will have the benefit of observing the important people in our world, because they will all be right in front of us. You're quiet, Hope. Penny for your thoughts?"

"Did you borrow that expression from Adelia, mom? She has a million of 'em."

"Let's say I borrowed this one for tonight…and just for you."

"I don't know how I am going to turn my mind away from Sydney and the horrible thing she experienced, and party with our loved ones. What about Sydney's loved ones? It seems like we have so much and she has nothing." Hope was in tears.

"Sweetheart, you are absolutely right, it is difficult to go from one extreme to another, especially when there is a vast space between the two. Sad and happy in Sydney's case are a million miles apart. In an adult world, we compartmentalize some of our work for another day. Let's save that for our teachable moments, when we listen and learn something from each other. What is it you call those times together? You heard it on a Honolulu radio station I believe."

"Brown Bags to Start 'em." Hope had nothing more to add.

"Close your eyes until we get home, sweetheart. You've had a very long day. I'll wake you when I'm close to our road."

"Sure."

And with her one-word response, Hope stretched out in her seat and quickly fell into a deep sleep.

As soon as Hope was asleep, Paradise took her foot off the gas pedal. There was not another car on the road so, while she could, Paradise slowed her car to twenty miles an hour and drove at that speed for maybe fifteen or twenty minutes. She was tired and anxious to be home, but she was driving at a snail's pace for a reason.

Paradise hadn't paid Adelia one cent for the food she was bringing to the party. *Or will she?*

Suddenly Paradise had doubts about her new friend. She didn't know the woman's last name, she didn't know her phone number, and she probably couldn't find her restaurant again even in daylight. *Please be real, Adelia. Please be real.*

As if on cue, a car caught up to Paradise and started flashing its high beams at her. Maybe it was Adelia, but most likely it was a stranger wondering who in God's name was driving twenty miles an hour on the only road in sight.

Paradise put her signal light on to turn right on to Cape St Mary Road. Watching in her rear view mirror, she smiled as she saw another right-turn signal light come on.

"Hope, wake up, sweetheart. We are almost home, and Adelia is right behind us."

"Why didn't you wake me up? I wanted to see how many cars were in Ben's yard."

"I looked for you, Hope: *one*, and it's Ben's car, with no lights on in the house. Dad wouldn't have invited him to our Cape party, would he?" Paradise was hoping it would not be an issue if Ben showed up.

"Mom, I was being totally honest when we discussed this before. I am too young to have a boyfriend, and I realize Ben is not too young, so he might be already taken by the time I graduate from high school. He said that will not be the case. His exact words were, 'You will be eighteen when you graduate from high school Hope. With your permission, I will pick you up for your senior prom.'"

Hope reached over to hug her mother. "Really, mom, I'm good. No worries if Ben is there. If he has a date, I will dig her eyes out, though."

It was nice to laugh.

"I swear to God, mother, every car in Cape St Mary is at our house. How blessed are we to live here with all these people who love us?"

Hope was in tears, but she didn't cry for very long. Lee had a habit of running straight to her side of the car and diving in to hug her, and she could see he was already coming her way.

She jumped out of the car and opened her arms wide. "Hello, little brother, did you miss me?"

"Did you bring food, Hope?"

"That was not the question, Lee. Did you miss me?"

"Yeah, but what about food?

Paradise joined the conversation. "Lee, the lady in the car right behind ours brought all the food for us. Her name is Adelia. Why don't you go to her car and ask if you can help her bring the food inside."

"Sure."

Lee was off Hope's lap and heading straight for Adelia. He had also picked up Hope's habit of one-word answers.

She reminded herself to be aware of everything she did and said around this smart little boy. His mind was like a sponge.

Thomas, Pops and Wilmot helped carry the baskets of food inside, and Adelia was beaming. She was certain she had thought of everything. She had pretty much used every bit of food in her restaurant. Tomorrow would be another day. She would worry about food tomorrow.

"You can help me empty the trunk, Paradise."

"There's more? Who are you? Who is this Adelia who is going to feed the masses?"

In the trunk, Adelia had a cold mini-fridge. "I forgot to ask how many young people would attend. Now and then we all need an ice cream, so I am never without this fridge. I also packed my mini hot plate that I will use to keep things warm once I set up inside. We are going inside, correct?" Adelia sensed that Paradise's mind was elsewhere just for a second.

"Follow me, Adelia. Welcome to our home with a combination of love, laughter and confusion that awaits us on the other side of this door. My kitchen is your kitchen. Come on in!"

~

And so another Cape party at #548 went on until 2 am. Delicious food! Lots to drink. Wonderful family and tons of friends. And retro music that brought everyone to the dance floor.

On the top step, just outside of Hope's bedroom and away from the eyes of the crowd, Hope and Paradise sat and observed their guests. First up for discussion was a lady making her first appearance at #548.

"I think Adelia must be an angel on earth," whispered Hope. "No human could put together a perfect menu in less than an hour, mom."

"I hope we have a new friend forever. Rave reviews about her food from all of our guests and the fact that she worked the entire evening serving the food was an over-the-top bonus. I'm with you, Hope. Adelia entered our lives today for a reason other than this evening."

Paradise was in awe of the woman. "We have got to go to her restaurant again soon. I hope you remember how to get there, because I do not. Adelia has certainly entertained and fed the masses here tonight. And now, like a fairy godmother, she is gone. Hope, are you with me? Tell me I haven't been talking to a sleeping girl."

Paradise reached over and softly gave Hope a wee shake.

"Mom, almost everyone has left and they are probably asleep in their own beds already. Dad is cleaning up right before our eyes. We can talk about all of our guests tomorrow but right now, I need sleep. I need my own bed."

"Go."

"Sure."

"Pardon?"

"Sure, mother, and thank you for taking me on this trip and thank you for—"

"Go."

Paradise kissed her daughter good night and went down stairs in pursuit of her handsome husband. Thomas was stretched out on the sofa, and Paradise decided to not wake him.

Covering him with a soft blanket, she kissed him lightly on the lips and then checked that all doors were locked. Within minutes Paradise was sleeping soundly in their bed.

45: Sydney's shadow

Thomas and Paradise sat on the window seat in their living room, watching the storm. The ocean's whitecaps seemed higher than an apartment building in the city. The storm was angry in its rage, yet mesmerizing at the same time. There had been little time to even think about watching the ocean since she and Hope had returned from Hawaii.

Footsteps on the stairs announced the arrival of either Hope or Lee. Given the early hour, it would most likely be Hope. Everyone enjoyed Lee's ability to sleep in every morning.

"Coffee fill-up, mom, dad?" Hope sat her mug down while she brought that second cup of morning coffee to her parents.

"Thank you, sweetheart, and good morning to you. I thought you might sleep a bit longer, given how late you went to bed."

"I'm young. What can I say?" Hope poured her coffee before continuing. "Mom, I heard you talking about Sydney. Have you spoken to her this morning? Do you think I could speak to her for a few minutes the next time you call her? I thought about her all night long, and the terrible things she had to endure to stay alive. What a brave woman she is. Honestly, when I think of all the things I have whined about in my life, I feel like a bit of a slug this morning. Maybe more caffeine will help. Last one for the day, I promise. You have to start somewhere, right, dad?"

"Hope," Thomas said, "listening to you talk about all the horrible things that bastard did to Sydney, and how you were thinking about her all night long, I'm worried that we made a mistake in exposing you to the details of such a violent attack on a woman. The fact that Sydney shared much of her experience with you and your mother speaks volumes. She allowed you into her safe space and asked you to spend the night so she could have more time with your mom. Sydney trusts you and your mom very much."

Continuing to think out loud Thomas said, "Both your mom and I are, or were, under contract with Sydney to—"

Paradise felt the need to jump in to make sure Thomas didn't share too much. "Thomas, you should know that Sydney had her assistant spend the afternoon with Hope, so we didn't drag her through all of the details. Lois, the assistant, was great and even brought all of the papers Sydney had promised to send to Hope. Speaking of that, did you know our girl is now setting her sights on becoming a forensic scientist? Sydney has taken Hope under her wing, right, Hope?"

"Roger that."

Hope was out of her chair and heading upstairs. Within minutes she returned with her dad's old briefcase, now hers, so she could show her parents all the documents Lois had given her. On the first page, Lois added her office number, her private office number and her home number.

"She knows I can keep a secret. See all of the phone numbers she has given me? Before either of you say it, I won't 'abuse her generosity,' I promise. I realize I saw and heard more over the last few days than your average teenager might see in a lifetime but, dad, knowing mom, we will be working on a new project together very soon. This will be all-consuming, so I will have other things to occupy my mind. I will never forget how broken and battered Sydney is, though. I promised her that."

Jumping in, Paradise did not disappoint. "Yes, Hope, you know me so well. I do have a project for us to work on. We started to discuss it before we stopped for food and met Adelia. You and I have to find Adelia's restaurant and take her a little gift."

"Sure. Don't worry, mom, I think Adelia is somewhere just around the corner."

Hope had relocated to the floor so she could spread out around her, by chapter title, everything she had been given. "Lois said that these documents are not in any particular order, and there will be no exam once I have finished reading everything. But check this out: thirteen thick documents on different topics related to forensic stuff. Maybe I'll begin by giving my personal project on this a more official title than 'forensic stuff.' I'll work on that."

"Speaking about what's 'around the corner' ladies," Thomas said, "things got a bit testy between me and Lee's two uncles while you were with Sydney. It's not a problem, but I do want you to be aware. I'm sure Lee will mention it."

"Should we be worried, dad?"

"Thomas, we both have time now. Could you fill us in?" Paradise could see that this was weighing heavily on him and she couldn't imagine what it might be.

"Of course. I didn't mean for it to sound so harsh. Denis and Waine have asked if Lee could travel to Honolulu with them to meet his 'other family' and see where his mother lived when she was his age."

Thomas paused to put a tad more cream in his coffee. "Denis is really the one I have talked with. He feels that if he shares the possibility of Lee spending any amount of time with his other family, meaning away from us, Waine might have a mental health episode if the trip does not happen. Denis was telling me that he never tells Waine about any trips they are taking until the morning when he can have the tickets, or a picture of the tickets, by Waine's place at the kitchen table. Denis really has taken on full responsibility for his brother. I admire him for that. I would also trust Denis to keep

Lee safe if we choose to let this trip happen. I'm so sorry for being so long winded…thoughts, ladies?"

Knowing her mother was not happy with this news, judging from the angry look on her face, Hope decided she would take a back seat and possibly slink out of the room if there was an opportunity to do so. Clearly this was adult stuff.

No one spoke immediately. Hope looked at her mother, who was staring at *her* and maybe even taking time to formulate what she wanted to say…to her own kid!

"Hope, I realize you haven't had any time to react but I'm going to ask you to tell your dad and me what your early thoughts are, because I need to discuss this with your dad privately. So share your thoughts then leave the room, sweetheart."

"Absolutely. I won't mind leaving the room at all. This is not news to me. I have heard both Denis and Waine bring Lee into a discussion about his possible visit to Hawaii."

Hope could see her comment didn't nothing to quell the rage on her mother's face. "Denis and Waine talk about showing their nephew where he is from and who his Hawaiian family is. I suspect there are many Hawaiian traditions they would also like to share with Lee. Many others, like Pops for example, have wondered aloud 'just how long it might be before Lee wants to learn about his mother's culture.' There really isn't anything wrong with that. I can go with them, if you like, as long as it's outside of the school year. I will excuse myself with that and will be in my room, door shut, reading my forensic files."

Seeing that her mother was already in tears, Hope did her best to lighten the mood. "Good luck to both of you with this discussion. Play fair. And remember to hold hands when you walk on the beach later. Be kind with each other. Talk it out."

"Go," from her father.

"Go," from her mother, using her outside voice.

Both parents were smiling, so Hope took that as a win. With her arms full of papers, she took the stairs, two at a time.

46: Wikolia

"Lee will never travel to Hawaii without me," Paradise said. "He needs his mother for the foreseeable future. I know Lee loves his uncles, Thomas, our son spends too much time with them. There is little discipline in Cabin #3 and that's good news for a five-year-old. Do you think Denis and Waine would settle for the four of us arriving on their doorstep for Christmas in Hawaii? Maybe we could make the trip as early as this year?"

Thomas knew this would be a hard sell, but the time was right to address it. The request would not go away. He wanted to ensure Paradise heard this from him, not from the uncles or anyone else who might bring it up.

He had been surprised to hear Hope talk about a possible trip for Lee. Clearly she had discussed this with her uncles, and with Lee, too. Denis and Waine talked about this quite openly and much of it was without any of the details but still…it was hanging over all of their heads.

"Denis and Waine are not at all interested in *us* going along on Lee's visit back to Hawaii. You are assuming they might already be back in Hawaii, Paradise, and I know that will not happen anytime soon, and it might not happen at all. They are both perfectly comfortable in Cabin #3."

Thomas could see how upsetting this was for Paradise, but he wanted her to have all the facts. "Denis brought this up when he first asked me about the *possibility* of taking Lee to the Island. They had no plans to go back home permanently. The brothers want to introduce Lee to the island as *they know it.* They are eager to talk with Lee about where his mother was born, where she grew up, and where he was born, as well. Lee has no memory of living with his mother. I think he tries to remember and this is how the idea first came up. Paradise, in the same conversation, Denis said that he knows Lee acts out of control around him and Waine. He said things would definitely change if they took him for a visit."

Thomas could see that Paradise was not taking this well, but there was more. "I have to be totally honest. A part of me wants to allow this to happen to honour the memory of his mother. As a family of four we talk openly about Wikolia, Lee's mother in Heaven, and we hear Lee comment that he looks 'a bit' like his uncles. He clearly does not remember what his mother looked like. He knows that we went on a road trip to see if we could find any members of Lee's family. Never did we think that Uncle Denis and Uncle Waine would find us instead! I think they will be waiting for an answer, now that you and Hope are back home. They will want to talk with both of us, and they will be happy to answer all your questions and a few more of mine I'm sure."

As if on cue, a very small person entered the room. "Hi, mom. Hi, dad. My uncles need to go and buy groceries, so they're not coming in with me. They are going to pick me up later because we have boxing matches booked at the Club. Where's my sister?"

"You give us both a big hug and I will tell you where she is," said Paradise, as she opened her arms wide.

Lee ran to his mother but stopped just inches away from her. "You're bawling. Why are you bawling, mommy? Are you sick or something?"

He jumped into her arms and gave her the biggest hug ever. "Maybe you should tell daddy why you're crying because when I cry, he always makes it better."

With that comment, Lee moved over to his dad. "You didn't make mommy bawl, did you, daddy? Can you fix her? You can do it just like you make all of my tears go away, right? Good luck with her, though, because she's bawling so hard her face is bigger and red and her eyes have marks under them that she doesn't have when she isn't bawling. Now, can someone tell me where my sister is please?"

Both parents said, 'Try her room, Lee. That's always a good place to start."

"Roger that."

"Wonder who he learned that from?" Thomas said. He took his wife's hand. "Talk to me, beautiful lady."

"I think I've been patient, but now the floor is mine. First of all, I feel that everyone, including you, Thomas, is ganging up on me. I seem to be the last to know anything about this. Why have I not heard what the uncles are planning before today? I'm Lee's mother, for God sake, Thomas, so why have you been keeping this from me? *Especially you?"*

If it was possible to cry for the entire day, Thomas feared that might be the case and he was scrambling to know what to say to help Paradise get back on track. She was making this about her, and that was not the case at all.

"Yes, you are Lee's mother. Like it or not, when Wikolia was alive, she, *not you,* was his mother. I remember you throwing that in my face a few times when I was struggling with working the night shift at 2.0 and raising my son during the day. Paradise, you will recall that, whenever I mentioned anything, anything at all, about Lee, your reply was either, 'Lee is *your* son,' or the one that always broke my heart, '*Lee is not my son*.'"

"I'm too emotional to talk about *our* son, so is it okay if we park this discussion for a few hours and talk about something else? Our contract with Sydney, maybe? I could bring you up to date about my meeting with her."

"Of course it's okay to park our discussion, but it won't go away."

47: Around the corner

"Thomas," Paradise said, "I was truly stunned with the morbid details Sydney shared in front of Hope. I had assumed we would keep it fairly light until Lois and Hope left the room. I was wrong. Sydney actually delved into the beatings, the rapes, the taunting and, of course, the gun. We spent the entire day on everything Sydney had been through. I explained to Hope that Sydney and I were not able to get all of our work done in one day, so we would sleep in one of her guest wings, finish up first thing in the morning then head home. Hope seemed fine with all of it, but now I'm not so sure."

Paradise indicated it was her husband's turn. She needed a minute.

"Don't underestimate our girl. Hope is mature beyond her years, and more so every day."

Thomas paused, but not for long. "This is only slightly off topic, but I would love to know how you were able to have us reinstated and still on contract with Sydney, almost as if she hadn't just fired us. There's no way she could have forgotten her outburst at our expense. She basically said, 'you're fired, so get out. *Get out now.*' I wish I had been with you when she shared that we were indeed on her payroll and in fact we had never been taken off the payroll. I'm also anxious to find out how that bastard escaped, so we can go back to Sydney with that information, if nothing more."

"Thomas, at the moment, Sydney is skittish around men...all

men. She jumps when a male member of her own staff comes to the house at her request. She jumps when her mental health expert, Doctor Langille, comes through the door. I will say, though, that the instant she sees his face you can see her body relax. Remember his name, because I predict that one day, not today but in the future, Doctor Langille will refer his file labelled *Doctor SS* to a colleague and begin to see our good Doctor Scott on a personal level."

"What are you saying?"

"It's early days, my love, but don't you forget what I've predicted."

Paradise stood for a few minutes blaming it on her back. Thomas knew better...his wife always stood when presenting something she might not yet be comfortable with.

"Thomas, I'm wearing my PI hat when I ask, 'Are we ready to begin our search for Sydney's daughter? Just before Hope and I left, Sydney said she needs me to go back soon to address what she wants of me in this exercise. She has shared with me that while she was being violated the man she would later murder talked repeatedly about where 'their daughter' lives. He also claimed he once introduced himself to her as a 'friend of your mother.' Thomas, while Sydney was slipping in and out of consciousness he claimed that he and their daughter have been in close touch all through her adult life, and that she wanted absolutely nothing to do with her mother. Sydney needed a couple of hours to share what I have just shared with you. It was as if she was in a trance and fighting with her mind and her body to release every word in her head and on her mind. I know I still have work to do to ensure I do not get involved emotionally with clients, but Sydney's words about her daughter not wanting to see her broke her heart, and it broke mine hearing her repeat it."

Paradise seemed to struggle with what she wanted to say next.

"Thomas, given what Sydney has been through, she has asked that, going forward, she will meet with me. Not with *us,* only *me.* She knows that often the work done behind the scenes is the most difficult, and she assumes that's what you will be working on. I believe Sydney either knows or has some vague idea where her daughter is, and that's the main reason I want to meet with her again. I hate to be the messenger with all of this, my love."

"Paradise, I have been expecting this. Did you notice how skittish Sydney was, with me in particular, when we appeared on her doorstep? She was so badly beaten, and her ability to recover in body and mind have only just begun. I don't take it personally, I'm sure she is the same way with most men at the moment...if not all. I also think she needs to blame one of us for not capturing the bastard before he got to her door. She's not wrong in thinking that way. We were to keep tabs on him at all times and we failed her. Believe me, I have gotten in the face of the warden at the prison, and have tracked down the member of our legislature for that area. I know the province has any number of government officials, so I wanted to ensure I had the right one. They don't make it easy. I see him next week. Bottom line is that our guy was *not to be released* pending his discovery and trial. I don't believe the warden was involved, so I am inclined to lean on parliamentary types. I'm not pointing fingers in advance of learning the truth but, between you and me, I suspect that what we are seeing is the reach of the long arm of the law. Breaking into something like this will take time, but we *wil*l get answers."

Paradise showed her stand-by-your-man face when reassuring Thomas that he was no more to blame than she was.

But Thomas couldn't let that go. "You were half a world away, at the deathbed of a friend. From the second we returned home from Sydney's that first time, when she told us what had happened to her, I have been working the phones and visiting people I thought could help me put a finger on the exact person who was ultimately in charge the day the man whose name we have never spoken walked out of his cell, out of the prison and, we believe, behind the wheel of a stolen car that was waiting for him, key in the ignition. The car was hidden to one side of the prison walls; he could not see it as he exited the final prison gate, yet he knew which way to turn. He had a partner in crime—I'm certain of it. We know now that he was going after Sydney. Paradise, something this significant has to be a 'fail' on someone's report card. If it's the last thing I do, I will get answers for Sydney. In the interim I will wear the 'fail.'"

~

"New topic," said Paradise.

Thomas nodded his approval.

"I can't believe that Hope and I walked into Adelia's little café and met an angel on earth. Or perhaps she is a magician who turned everything in her café into finger food in the blink of an eye. Hope and I are going to go up the line one day, and we are not coming home until we find her."

Paradise smiled at Thomas before she added, "Or at least until it gets dark. *You are my driver after dark.*"

"And happy to wear that hat for you."

Over the next forty-five minutes Paradise had Thomas laughing out loud as she went into each detail. He could see the huge dish of french fries and he could almost taste how delicious they were.

"Paradise, I almost hate to ask. At the very least, do you know Adelia's last name?"

Paradise shook her head from side to side. No last name.

"Actually I might have a lead on her last name, said Thomas. "I had a wonderful discussion with her as she warmed up some of her finger foods. Adelia shared how she and her small friends once played here, in 548, and she would continue to visit this address, in its original state, for many years. Her grandfather's last name was *Ambrose*, so we will start there."

"Smart and handsome." Paradise was enjoying this.

"Do you remember which exit you took off the highway?"

"That would be *no*."

"Do you remember the name of Adelia's café? Please say, yes."

"Yes that I do know: Adelia's Café." Laughter all around.

"Before you and Hope go weaving on and off the highway, remember you and I are PIs. Surely to God we can get you an address before you leave home. I'll start there when I have a second or two. In fact, let's make this an excursion, and take a family day trip up the line. I'm sure the four of us can find Adelia!"

Paradise nodded, in the affirmative this time. *Good sign*, thought Thomas.

~

"Paradise, have you noticed that Pops seems to be fading away before our eyes? He hasn't mentioned any new health issue to you, has he? Other than his bride, of course, you would be his second confidante, I think." Thomas didn't want to worry Paradise, but he thought Pops should see a doctor.

"I brought it up with him at the café again yesterday, and it was *not* pretty. He got quite huffy, in fact."

> "Now, why in God's name would I pay good money to see a doctor? I'm officially old, as you and Paradise damn well know. Christ, man, you see me every day. What do you think is wrong with me other than my bones ache and I'm falling apart?"
>
> Pops paused in thought for a moment, then said, "I'll tell you what I will do, if it will get you off my back, Eugenie has a doctor's appointment coming up soon, and instead of

> simply going to the office with her, I will see if I can make my feet actually go *in* with her when they call her name. No promises though."

"Putting his cap on and standing ramrod straight Pops made sure I realized the conversation was over. He leaned my way and with the tiniest of smiles, I could see his mind churning. 'You tell Paradise that you just pissed me off!'"

Paradise said, "I am ashamed to say I hardly saw either Pops or Eugenie at our latest party. Have you mentioned your concern to Eugenie? She might know something we don't. That doesn't mean she would share it with me. She is very protective of her 'groom', as she continues to call Pops."

"No, I have not brought it up with Eugenie. I figure that's your job, since you're much closer with her than I am."

"Roger that. Leave it with me."

~

"Speaking of family," said Paradise some time later, "my brother, Wilmot, and his lady, Marie, are looking well. I spent some time with them last evening and learned more than I will ever need to know about Rescuee, their dog. That dog is good for the both of them, I think. I asked if they were still content in their small cottage. 'Yes, we are,' Marie said. 'It's perfect for us. Neither of us needs a home with rooms we don't use and have to be dusted.'"

It was a known fact that Marie wasn't one to stay inside and do housework when Rescuee gave her multiple reasons to head down to Mavillette Beach for a long walk.

Paradise made a mental note to touch base with Wilmot, maybe Marie, too, tomorrow if not today. They had both suffered major trauma to their bodies. She wanted to ensure they were still meeting with their doctors.

~

Sitting in a fancy Italian restaurant a world away in Honolulu, Hawaii, dressed to the nines, and drinking the finest of Champagnes, Lieutenant Commander Jalen Lexis held Bonde's hand. "Beautiful lady, I have a proposition for you."

He knew Bonde would interrupt, "A proposition? Sir, you're already sleeping with me, so I'm anxious to hear what's left in terms of a proposition."

Bonde knew her guy, as she called him, would let her interrupt. He did not disappoint. He had also allowed her to call him 'Sir.' Bonde had a way about her. She mesmerized him.

Jalen realized they were moving fast. Too fast for his comfort level, but he was 'going with the flow' as Bonde had called it when he brought it up during one of their late night calls. If they didn't sleep in the same room, they were on the phone with each other.

"I know you're eager to return to work, Bonde. I know you will always need your own money, and God knows you won't take any from me. Before returning to work, let me take you away on a vacation...totally my treat. You can't even bring a wallet. I can see you're itching to interrupt me, but I'm not going to let you have the floor until I finish. Enjoy your Champagne, lean back, and just listen. Please."

"Yes, sir! I'm leaning back with Champagne in hand. Please continue."

"I haven't taken a vacation since my good wife passed away, over a decade ago. I need a vacation, Bonde. Let's fly to Nova Scotia, rent a car, and make a road trip to Cape St Mary. We can explore Canada, if you like, but let's get to the Cape first and figure things out from there. What do you think?"

"Sir, before I say yes can you clarify if we are talking a couple of weeks or a couple of months? I could rent my house here and that would cover my bills while I'm away."

"Let's say at *least* a couple of months. I think you are more likely to find a good person or family if you rent your place out for six months. If you do that, we could figure something out if we are back here before that period ends. I will make sure you're not left out in the cold."

"Sir, you have told me more than once that you loved the fact that I'm always keen to check out what's around the corner. I'm all in, let's do it."

With a sexy salute Bonde concluded with, "Sir!"

"Perfect, thanks for trusting me with this. I will give my travel agent some details and see when we should fly to Canada, weather-wise. I'm not ready for snow, so I need to be reminded when it is the warmest, in Nova Scotia in particular."

Bonde picked up her empty champagne glass, nodding for a refill. With both of their glasses topped up, she said, "Here's to finding ourselves in Nova Scotia, Canada."

"I'll drink to that."

Jalen wanted to say something like 'that was easy', but Bonde might change her mind about the trip and he wasn't taking any chances.

~

The PIs in Cape St Mary went to work. "I'm off to see the prison warden again," said Thomas. "This time my objective will be to speak with cell mates, and anyone else at the jail who knew X, as we're going to call him, or who had heard anything about him.

Thomas was also anxious to see if there was any chatter about X being alive or dead. Nothing had been leaked, and that in itself was worth investigating. That would mean calling Sydney, so Thomas would speak with the Warden first.

Next, one of the PIs would need to talk with Sydney before they went to the Chief of Police. Someone had ordered 'no press and no internal leaks of this information' and the PIs wanted to know who the top person involved in this would be.

"I'll call Sydney to check in and check up on her," Paradise said. "She said that she knows she has actually preformed autopsies on women X raped and killed. The families of the deceased might know something we don't. Additionally I'm going to search for any of the young women X raped but did not murder. They might remember something if we can find them and convince them to speak with us."

"Good ideas."

"I need to book a date with Sydney," Paradise said, "but I would love to have some Intel concerning her daughter. Let's open a file for 'Miss Scott'."

"'Miss S', just to be safe," offered Thomas.

Paradise pulled out a new journal. Making notes always helped her think more clearly. She gave the journal the title of 'Miss S.' On the last page she simply put a big 'X.'

Above all else, Paradise offered a silent prayer. "Dear Lord in Heaven, please help us find justice for Nova Scotia's Chief Coroner, Doctor Sydney Scott."

~

"Thomas," Paradise said, "did our daughter tell you she wants to join our PI company when she graduates from university? Hope's goal, at sixteen, so this might change, is to be a private investigator but with a twist. She has her sights set on becoming a forensic investigator. When I asked her to explain what that would entail she said, and I quote, 'Science + the Justice System = Forensics.' I think she is in awe of Sydney and that's making her determined to be more than a regular PI. Her words, not mine."

"We better see a definite upswing in our PI work, because Hope's education could cost a small fortune."

Thomas was wringing his hands as he spoke. "I can't even imagine how many years of education she would require. Something this important to Hope makes me wonder why she has not shared this with me. This is dinner table talk, with all of us enjoying her excitement as she shares her goals."

"Hope and I have had hours involving what we call windshield time driving from here to Halifax and back more than a few times together in the last while, and some eleven hours of airplane windshield time from Halifax to Hawaii and home again. Windshield time doesn't require you to look directly at the person you are talking with. People sometimes share their dreams during windshield time. There are no boundaries. Trust me Thomas, you will hear everything Hope is learning about forensics."

"If Hope is serious about this, and grade ten is a good time to at least begin to think seriously about post high school education, we are going to have some intellectual discussions over supper."

"Thomas! I can't wait to see where this goes."

"And I guess many of the 'papers' Hope received from Sydney's assistant, Lois, are forensics related, right, Paradise?" Thomas was smiling, while already worrying about how they would be able to cover all the costs associated with more than one university degree.

"Roger that."

Without much thought Paradise decided to throw another idea out there for discussion. "Thomas, we might want to think about moving to Halifax, or maybe having a small place in the city, if that is where Hope finds the university she hopes to attend." Paradise could see that she was losing Thomas. "Sorry, honey, I've gotten carried away with things that are at least three years away, so lots of time to worry and plan and save."

Thomas breathed a sigh of relief. "My God, girl, you took my breath away with your, 'we might have to move to the city' idea. You're not thinking of selling our home, are you?"

"I know, and I'm sorry," said Paradise. "We have enough on our plates at the moment."

"You have nothing to be sorry for. Funny enough, during my most recent call with Clint and Jim, we talked about the split of the cases we have, and I offered that, once we put the final stamp on our Doctor SS and Miss S files, I can take some cases requiring immediate attention. I might have to fly to Toronto and then drive up to Port Hope for at least one meeting with our partners."

~

Hope could hear her parents talking about Sydney and kids and work and bills. *They're were catching up on everything going on in our family.*

Normally she would join them, but not today. "Hey, this sounds kind of heavy. I'm off for a walk, but I won't be long."

Without waiting for a response, Hope was out the back door, walking down Cape St Mary Road until she reached the cottage at #8. The last time Hope had knocked on this door she left with a broken heart.

Knocking *without* opening the door seemed to be a better decision than opening the door herself. *Fool me once...*

"Hope?" Ben was stunned. He had not laid eyes on Hope since forever.

"Can I come in, or are you entertaining another woman? One who doesn't drive?"

Hope was smiling as she made light of the 'Danielle-day' joke she had created for her thoughts only. Plus there, was just Ben's car near the house.

"Where are my manners? Yes, of course, Hope, please come in. Is everything okay with your family? You're not sick are you? Are you eighteen already? When's the prom?"

Ben had her laughing out loud and nothing had ever sounded so sweet. "What can I get you?"

Hope took a quick look around the kitchen and sat on what seemed to be the only chair in the room. "Can I have a soda? I didn't think you would ever stop with the questions. Ben, I've missed this...friendship."

"Sure." Ben's reply came with a second chair, a fold-up chair, coming out of nowhere, but at least he was eye-level with Hope now. "I have missed staring into your beautiful eyes, young lady."

"Ben, I have a question for you, and it's a serious one, so don't reply like I'm some sixteen-year-old who isn't serious."

This gave Ben hope that she might be his girlfriend once again... and without the three-year wait. He leaned forward, pretending he didn't know this was all about their relationship. "Talk to me, Hope. Spill it all out."

"What do you know about forensic science?"

The end

Acknowledgements

- Brenda Thompson, founder of Moose House Publications, and Andrew Wetmore, editor, I have so much respect for the work you do to help all of your authors. Thank you for giving my books a home.
- Thank you to Nicole Ruuska, who painted the cover for this book. During the summer you might see Nicole at the Artist Shack in Margaretsville. www.nicoleruukas.com
- *Thank you for being a friend* to all fans of the Paradise Series. I appreciate you.

Claudette d'Entremont arrived at Coles in Yarmouth with a question. "I have all of your books in the Paradise Series. Could you sign my four copies?"

"Yes, I can."

hanks also to photographer Margaret d'Entremont.

About the author

Carol Ann Cole is a best-selling author, a professional speaker and the founder of the Comfort Heart Initiative. *Around the Corner with Paradise is* her fifth fiction in The Paradise Series.

Learning to Slow Dance with Footprints of Kindness will be Carol Ann's fifth non-fiction book. Moose House is due to release it in 2023.

Already a Member of the Order of Canada, Carol Ann has also received the Terry Fox citation of honour, the Hope Award, and inclusion in the McLean's Honour Roll, to name a few of her awards.

Carol Ann spends time in both Halifax and Toronto.

Printed in the USA
CPSIA information can be obtained
at www.ICGtesting.com
BVHW051707030823
668190BV00018B/168

9 781990 187926